The Eagle
and
The Hart

by

Maggie Shaw

The Eagle
and
The Hart

by

Maggie Shaw

eregendal.com

Also by the Author

The Vision and Beyond (2018)
Diviner's Nemesis I – Avenger (2019)
Diviner's Nemesis II – Retribution (2020)
The Eagle and The Butterfly (2020)
The Last Thursday Ritual in Little Piddlington (2021)
The Eagle and The Raven (2021)
Waiting for the Dawn (2022)
The Teddies of Rosehill Cottage (2022)

First published in the United Kingdom in 2022 by
Eregendal.com, Rosehill Road, Crewe, Cheshire, CW2
8AR. Printed in the United Kingdom by Lulu.com.

ISBN 978-1-7397801-4-2 (paperback)

Contents

Introduction
and Acknowledgements

The Eagle and The Hart opens as Imperial Knight and Ministerialis Gendal tells Oscar, Prince of Harzland, that his older brother Rehlein is dead. But things are not as they seem in Harzberg, and Gendal stays to find out why. Unravelling the mystery of the death of Oscar's father, Prince Umbert, culminates in a deadly battle in the very hall where the old Prince had died. This story of court politics, power play and warfare in a medieval German princedom, is the third novel in the Knight Gendal series of historical adventures. With twists aplenty, it will keep readers guessing until the last page.

Even though a novel of this sort is a work of fiction, a lot of research is required to create an authentic medieval world view for the reader. My reference sources included *The Time Travellers Guide to Medieval England* by Ian Mortimer (2008) and *The Complete Book of Heraldry* by Stephen Slater (2002), the website www.arms-n-armor.com and several Facebook groups dedicated to the exchange of information about medieval culture and warfare. Practical research included a session with the School of Historical Combat in Moseley and historical re-enactments such as the Medieval Joust held by English Heritage at Beeston Castle. I am very grateful to all who have shared their knowledge and skills through both discussion and demonstration.

As always, I would like to thank those who helped with the book in any way, especially the late Roy Butler for his assistance with the story. Thanks also to Eregendal's social media followers, who gave useful guidance in the choice of cover design. Any faults in the work are my own alone.

Characters

Aglé Moltké	Young maiden in Oscar's court, pursues Gendal
Albrecht	Duke of Romfeld; withdrew fiefs from Arnulf and Opecz
Arnulf Althaus	Lord, courtier in Prince Oscar's court
Cara Rea	Marie of Burgundy's alias: she once betrayed Gendal
Dietl	Steward at Rehberg Castle
Eleanore	wife of Prince Oscar, former family Boesel
Eregendal	The younger idealistic Gendal
Finstar	Gendal's horse, a black stallion
Gendal	Free Knight, Ministerialis, the one telling the story
Goswin	Page assigned to Gendal at Harzberg
Heinrich	Uncle to Prince Oscar: brother of his mother
Herlinde	Oscar and Sigmund's mother
Hirschmann	Sigmund and Oscar's family name
Ilse	Sinter's mother and Volkmar's wife
Imperator	The Emperor of the Holy Roman Empire
Irmel	Wise woman, protected by the brigands
John Silvio	John O' The Woods, brigand leader
Klaus	Young knight who supports Gendal, relative of Herlinde
Louis	King of Rome, campaigning to be elected Imperator
Marlena Moltké	Young maiden in Oscar's court; betrothed to Sinter
Matthias	Cistercian monk; physician and apothecary
Nicolaus	Duke of Danuvia, cousin to the Imperator
Opecz	Lord, courtier in Prince Oscar's court, Sheriff of Harzberg
Oscar	Prince of Harzland; Rehlein's younger brother
Petrus	Doctor: Sigmund and Oscar's former tutor at Rehschloss
Rehlein	Gendal's travelling friend, prince of Harzland
Schwarzenberg	Volkmar and Sinter's family name
Sigmund	Prince of Harzland: Rehlein's real name
Sinter	Prince, Sigmund's cousin and co-conspirator
Umbert	Prince of Harzland: Rehlein and Oscar's murdered father
Volkmar	Prince of Schwarzenberg; Sinter's father

Chapter 1
The Letter and The Ring

The letter burned in my pocket as the massive castle gates swung open for me. I rode through the archway between the gatehouse towers into the grassy ward. A page took the head of my black horse Finstar and led us across the cobbled courtyard to the Great Hall, a stone building built against the curtain wall. As I dismounted, I looked up to see a face watching me from a window of the royal apartments above. I handed Finstar's reins to the page, who led him away to the stables.

In the doorway at the top of the steps to the Great Hall stood a seasoned knight wearing the red and white Hart surcoat of Harzland. He had thick grizzled hair, a weathered face and a distinctive black and white beard. The confidence in his stance made him seem to fill the open doorway.

'You have a message for Prince Oscar? I am his uncle, Lord Heinrich. I will take it to him.'

'I am Imperial Knight Gendal. I have been instructed to hand the letter I carry to Prince Oscar in person,' I replied.

He scowled and would have objected, but for the ring on my hand bearing the authority of our last Imperator.

'If you must! Follow me.'

He turned without courtesy and led me into the Great Hall.

It felt a relief to be inside a solid building after my long winter ride from Aacheim. As Heinrich left to find Oscar, I looked at the weapons displayed on the stone walls: wheels of swords in fashions old and new, and rows of shields emblazoned with the Hart of Harzland: the same red hart's head against a white field. To see such a display outside the armoury suggested this principality believed its battles had all been in the past. I recalled the prosperous streets I had ridden through in the city, the well-fed faces, the happy children and the absence of beggars. This wealthy land would be a tempting acquisition for an empire-building leader from a more martial nation.

'Knight Gendal,' greeted Oscar as he came into the hall.

He took his seat in the large carver chair which stood on the dais at the head of the chamber. Heinrich sat beside him where he had indicated, on a plainer chair. When they had settled, he beckoned me forward. I bowed and crossed the hall to the foot of the dais.

'Your Highness, your brother, Prince Rehlein, instructed me to bring you these items in the event of his death,' I said with compassion as I offered him the letter and the ring in my right hand.

Oscar shook his head and frowned, a bemused smile on his complacent face. He looked so like Rehlein: a younger, less physically fit version; blond, blue eyed, well-fed.

'But I do not have a brother called Rehlein,' he said, and smirked at Heinrich.

I thought quickly as I bowed to acknowledge his response. Grief can take many forms, but this did not seem like one of them.

'Prince Oscar, I have this letter and this ring to give you. I was commissioned to bring them to your Highness by a Prince who called you his brother, and who called Sinter Schwarzenberg his second cousin, and who used the travelling name Rehlein.'

The smug look dropped from his face.

'And you say he is dead?'

'He died a hero's death, fighting for justice and freedom.'

'Then he died a fool.'

But Oscar did hold out his hand to take the letter and the ring. He paled as he rotated the ring in his right hand and fingered its seal etched with the Hart of Harzland.

'Did you see him fall?' he asked me, looking only at the ring.

'No. He fell in the heat of battle. I saw his body on the ground, his armour and mail. His head was at a curious angle. It looked as if he had fallen from his horse and broken his neck.'

'So you have no actual proof. When did this happen?'

'The 27th of September, two months ago, at the Battle of Dernfels in Danuvia.'

'But it is now December. What delayed you in completing his commission?'

'Duke Nicolaus took me as his prisoner of war. I did not escape until Mischief Night and Halloween.'

Oscar nodded and lowered his head to read more of the letter.

'By your leave, Prince Oscar,' said Heinrich as he cast a critical eye over me. 'Gendal is an unusual name in these parts, but we have heard of that name before. I recall a messenger called Gendal who caused your mother great heartache, while you and your brother were still youths. The messenger caused Prince Sigmund to abscond when he left us that first time.' He glared at me. 'Was that you?'

'Rehlein and I did travel together on a quest some years ago, with two others, shortly after I had been accepted by the Guild of Guides and Messengers.'

'When did Sigmund give you this letter and commission?' Oscar asked.

'It was the night before our army set out for Dernfels, four days before the battle. He had a gloom upon him, as if he had had a premonition.'

'According to this letter, you have been a good friend to my brother, Knight Gendal. I shall see you are well recompensed for your loyalty. Heinrich, arrange for Gendal to be given quarters, and assign a page.'

'As you wish, Prince Oscar.'

Heinrich bowed, his expression showing his distaste for the instructions. He left the Great Hall.

'Thank you, your Highness, for your hospitality,' I said and gave a respectful bow: 'Alas, I cannot stay long. I have to take the same sad news to Schwarzenberg. Prince Sinter also fell at Dernfels.'

'But you must come back here after,' Oscar urged. He chuckled. 'I see Heinrich is not very impressed with you. He remembers the hurt you caused his sister, my mother Lady Herlinde, the first time Sigmund disappeared from court. I can still remember my joy when my brother came back after his two years on the road with you. How he sang your praises! It made a powerful impression on me as a seventeen-year-old. Were you responsible for him leaving the second time too? We were all disappointed he did not stay long enough to attend my coronation.'

'No, not the second time. I happened upon him in my travels, and we journeyed together once more for old times' sake.'

My neutral reply hid my surprise at the content of Oscar's last words. If he had been seventeen when Rehlein had returned at about the age of twenty, why had Oscar been crowned Prince of Harzland and not Rehlein? Was this caused by the trouble that the heir apparent Rehlein had only hinted at during the few summer months we had travelled together again before he died?

Oscar regarded me thoughtfully, having noticed how I had dropped the convention of addressing him by title in my reply. The tense atmosphere my mistake had created was broken by Heinrich's return with a page. Oscar gave me permission to leave his presence and instructed the page to escort me to my quarters. As I bowed my way backwards out of the Great Hall, I saw the prince give Rehlein's letter to Heinrich to read.

Chapter 2
A Chance Meeting

The page took me to a bedchamber in the royal apartments above the Great Hall. My saddlebags had already been brought up to the room. When he offered to unpack them, I thanked him but refused.

'What is your name, page?' I asked.

'Goswin, Sir,' he said, looking downwards with flushed cheeks. He appeared to be about eleven years old, with sandy-blond hair, deep blue eyes, and a well-tanned face. He wore the livery of the castle, with the Hart tunic over an earthy linen shirt and breeches, and brown cloth shoes.

I could see he felt nervous in my presence. To help him become more at ease, I asked some simple questions about the castle and the Prince's family. He relaxed as he told me about meals, combat training sessions, and the other people with rooms in the Royal apartments. I listened while putting away my few possessions in a dark wooden press. The modern storage cupboard was beautifully carved with a pattern of intersecting arches. The carpenter who created it had great skill.

'How long have you been in the service of the Prince?' I asked.

'Since I was eight. The kitchens needed a handy lad.'

'You must have given good service to be a page now.'

He blushed. 'It's my first time, Sir. But I know what the other pages do. I'll do my best, Sir.'

'I can't ask you to do more.' I smiled to have discovered just what Heinrich thought of me. 'It must have been exciting to work in the kitchens, when Oscar was crowned.'

'Oh, it was, Sir,' Goswin agreed. His eyes shone with enthusiasm as he told me about the feast the kitchen had prepared and the guests who had attended. I did not recognise any of the names.

'Did Prince Sigmund attend?' I asked casually.

'No, Sir. Shall I show you round the castle?'

'Thank you. That would be good. I've already seen the Great Hall. Where should we go next?'

'The Lesser Hall, Sir: where Prince Umbert died.'

Goswin took me down the main staircase to the ground floor landing, from which two doors led off: one to the right and the Great Hall; the other to the left and the Lesser Hall. We entered the smaller hall through a curtained corner door, coming out near a cavernous disused fireplace in the short, windowless panelled wall. The corresponding wall opposite featured the musicians' gallery, a first-floor balcony accessed by a small door in the panelling which would be invisible when shut. The two long walls were hung with tapestries below the windows: oblong clerestory panels above the main doorway through the courtyard wall, and little more than arrow slits on the outer wall.

In front of the fireplace, stood a large refectory table flanked by two heavy benches and headed with carver chairs at the ends. Goswin crossed the floor to touch the chair nearer the door.

'This is where Prince Umbert died,' he said with reverence.

'Do you miss him?'

'He was a good man, Sir. Things haven't been the same since he went.'

'In what way?'

'I don't know, Sir. I just work in the kitchens usually. I don't get to know about that sort of thing.'

'Then let's go to the kitchens.'

Goswin led me out through the main doors into the cobbled courtyard part of the inner ward. All the principal structures in the castle had been built in stone against the outer walls. The kitchens stood apart from the other buildings to lessen the risk of fire.

Inside, the kitchens were dark and smoky. Goswin introduced me to his fellow workers. The cooks and hands made a fuss of him and treated me with respect, offering to find me something to eat before the evening meal. I declined and left them to their work.

The next building against the wall was a two-storey barracks with servants' quarters above and the royal stables beside.

'Prince Oscar has fifty household cavalry men,' Goswin said proudly: 'They will be coming back from training soon. The Castellan oversees them. He looks after the castle too.'

'I wonder if he would let me join their training session tomorrow?'

'I'm sure he will, Sir. He wants everyone to train with him. He says you can't be too careful. But I've never been able to go because I've always been too busy in the kitchens.'

'Perhaps that will change tomorrow.'

We called into the stable to check on Finstar. Then Goswin led me further round the wall to an arched gateway.

'This is the way to the gardens. Would you like to see them, Sir?'

I agreed and followed him through the inner wall into a south-facing walled garden. The first and largest section of the garden was a vegetable plot which had been dug over for the winter. A well-managed compost heap lay below the garderobe outlets. Beyond the vegetable plot stood several fruit trees, separating the vegetables from a herb garden. As we strolled out of the trees, I realised we were not alone there.

On the far side of the herb garden, a woman emerged from a small potting shed which had been built against the outer wall. She wore a green velvet gown and a white linen day hood. Around her lay neat beds laid out in a symmetrical pattern with gravel paths between, the plants tidily trimmed back for winter.

'Lady Herlinde,' whispered Goswin with wide eyes that told me we should not be there.

'You go back to the stables, Goswin. I will make our apologies.'

Goswin vanished among the fruit trees as I walked towards the widow, Oscar's and Sigmund's mother. We met by some conical wicker bee skeps, which stood in arched recesses in the outer wall.

Close to, Lady Herlinde's lined face looked old and tired. A tress of long grey hair had escaped her linen wimple, and her eyes were wet with tears. Though her velvet gown looked warm, she shivered in the weak winter sun. I bowed to her, averting my eyes from her show of sorrow.

'Please forgive me for intruding upon your solitude, Lady Herlinde,' I said, and bowed my head again to give her the respect of her situation.

'Who are you? And what are you doing here?' she asked. Her voice was deep and melodic: a voice which under other circumstances would calm the fiercest storm.

'I am Knight Gendal, newly arrived from Aacheim. I was exploring your fine castle, and did not think I would find anyone here.'

She turned away, her voice cracking as she said, 'I come here when I need to think.'

After regaining her self-control, she turned back. I saw the tears still brimming in her eyes as she spoke on.

'I must thank you, Knight Gendal, for bringing us the awful tidings of Sigmund's death. I have long wanted to meet you, but not in this way.'

She turned away again to hide the power of the emotions sweeping over her. I waited in silence until she faced me again to continue our conversation.

'Heinrich said my dear boy died in battle. Were you in the same company?'

'Yes, Ma'am. We both supported the Children of the Raven in Bavaria, in their fight against tyranny. Though we lost the battle, the Lord saw to it that the Raven won the war.'

'So he threw his life away.'

Despite my having heard her comment before from Oscar's lips, the way she said it made me see the loss from a new and unexpected viewpoint. Before I could respond, she spoke again, changing the subject as if the facts of Rehlein's death were too cruel to hear so soon.

'I used to resent you for taking my baby away from me. He was gone for two years, and we heard nothing. What made him leave with you?'

'We went on a quest, in search of truth. Sigmund was my third companion: one of the Four, all of us naïve cubs. I had just earned my licence from the Guild of Guides and Messengers and thought I knew it all.'

'Did you find this truth you were looking for?'

'Not the truth we sought, but we came across other truths. My companions eventually tired of the endless journey: one by one, each went their separate way. Some time later, I thought I saw Sigmund in a theatre crowd, but I wasn't sure as he had changed.'

'He had changed a lot when he came back to us after his time away with you. No longer did he despise our court and our wealth, and he understood why we rule Harzland the way we do.'

'What happened to make him leave here again?'

She stepped away; her face suggesting my question had confused her. I caught up with her and spoke to explain myself.

'This summer, I came across Sigmund drinking far too much in the Bush Inn in Strasbourg, in the company of a crowd of fair-weather friends. I dragged him away to save him from them and took him with me on my travels. Tragically, I saved his life there only to bring him to his death all the sooner, on the battlefield at Dernfels. The brightest star, he burned so fiercely, only to be snuffed out far too soon.'

She crouched down to pick two sprigs of mint and sage, symbols of wisdom and virtue. Their few winter leaves were some of the only greenery in the garden. The action gave her time to think about how to answer me. When she stood up, she looked me directly in the eye, her gaze filled with sorrow and anger.

'They accused him of murdering his father, my husband. On that cursed May Day, I lost the two men I loved the most.'

She thrust the posy of herbs into my hand. Then she fled sobbing from the herb garden towards the gate back into the castle ward. I let her go and stayed on among the herbs to think through the significance of her words and deeds. A movement made my eyes glance up at the castle wall. A face disappeared from a high window before I could identify who it might be.

Chapter 3
At the Training Lists

That evening, I dined with the family and their retinue in the Great Hall. Oscar honoured me with a place near the end of the top table, between the lean blond Chamberlain and the stout blond Castellan. Together, these two officials ran the royal household and the castle. The knights of the household cavalry headed the table to the right below us, with the rest of the household seated on the table to our left and further away in order of rank The cavalrymen wore their white surcoats emblazoned with the red Hart of Harzland, Oscar's heraldic design.

I had taken the precaution of instructing Goswin to draw me a jug of fresh water from the castle well to wash down my meal. My dinner companions were both enjoying the local wine. As the food served to us reflected the restrictions of Advent fasting, the wine dulled their senses faster than they were aware. Soon they had forgotten I was a relative stranger and chatted about household matters without reservation. Most of it was gossip and tittle-tattle: the sorts of things that happen in any community the size of Harzberg castle. The petty nature of much of their talk told me the castle, city and principality were well run and its citizens well cared for. When I told them the prosperity of Harzland was a delight to see after the poverty and greed I had witnessed and fought against in Danuvia earlier that year, they received the compliment with personal pride.

After an interesting exchange about some of the young knights eating at the table below, our conversation naturally drifted to the subject of their training and exercises.

'Would you allow me to join the household knights for training tomorrow?' I asked the Castellan: 'I've been travelling a lot and have lost some of my edge.'

He nodded expansively and rambled on about the need to keep one's strength and agility at peak performance.

'Unlike our beloved Prince,' said the Chamberlain with a sneer.

'Yes. At least Sigmund trained with our men once in a while to encourage them,' the Castellan returned. 'He couldn't keep it up, though. Soft, both of them. Not like their father. Now, he was a soldier prince!'

'I've heard tales of Prince Umbert. Did he ever compete in the tiltyard?' I asked.

'Compete? He loved jousting. No-one could better him, and it wasn't for the want of trying.'

'That was until he aged,' the Chamberlain said.

'True: he wasn't the man he used to be, towards the end,' the Castellan agreed.

'Was it through his ill health that Prince Oscar came by the throne?' I asked.

The Chamberlain gave me a sidelong glance. 'Prince Umbert died last May Day, during the entertainments.'

'Sigmund didn't want the responsibility: he still craved adventure,' said the Castellan. 'So Prince Oscar married Lady Eleanore and inherited the crown.'

I looked along the table to where Oscar sat. His wife was not beside him. To his right sat his mother Herlinde, and to his left his uncle Heinrich.

The Chamberlain saw the direction of my gaze and explained, 'Princess Eleanore is great with child. She chooses to eat with her ladies-in-waiting.'

'May God bless the fruit of their union,' I politely replied.

The conversation wound on into late evening. Convention required that the guests all stayed until Prince Oscar had left the table and the dining chamber. I was one of the first to leave after him. It was a pleasure to sleep in a feather bed in a warm room that night, after so many nights in seedy inns and woodland hollows.

Next morning, I joined the household cavalry in the cold, damp training field. Because it was customary to train with blunted weapons, I wore my black leather gambeson rather than my plated brigandine over my chain mail. The sleeveless padded leather jacket would protect me from the knocks and bruising I risked when training with warriors I had not met before. Goswin came with me to act as my page, ready to assist with weapons and fetch Finstar to me when required.

The fifty strong household cavalry troop marched out onto the training field on foot. They were clearly identifiable with their hart surcoats in red on white over their mail. They moved as a unit with the discipline and confidence born of regular training together.

For their opening exercise, the men paired up to spar with swords. The Castellan introduced me to some of them and explained their fighting moves as if I were a novice. I appreciated the caution of his approach to my training and let him continue without comment, preferring to prove my ability rather than claim it.

He paired me with a young knight to spar and watched as we blocked, parried and thrust at each other. I found the young man's moves easy to read and predict, and parried each one with little effort. When he failed to break through my guard at all, the Castellan replaced him with a more experienced knight. This warrior proved a better match for me, and we enjoyed sparring with each other. He helped me sharpen my reactions, and I trust I did the same for him.

Midmorning, the Castellan split us into two groups. The older group sparred with axes, while my mainly younger group punched straw-stuffed bags on poles to improve our general strength and fitness. After a short time, we took over the axes while the other group took over the punch bags. By noon, my whole body ached with the unusual exertion.

The household cavalry welcomed me to eat their lunch of pease pottage with them in the Greater Hall. Our break was over all too soon. The Castellan sent us all to the stables to saddle our horses for the afternoon session.

Goswin had already groomed and saddled Finstar for me and led my gleaming black stallion out into the courtyard. As was my habit, I checked over my horse and his tack, and found all in good order.

Thanks to Goswin's efforts, we were among the first to arrive for lance practice. I had rarely used a lance in my travels and found this the toughest part of the training that day. The first exercise comprised cantering along the wooden tilt wall with lance held forward in my right hand across Finstar's shoulder, to spear rings hung on hooked poles to my left along the tilt. Those of us who hooked the rings consistently went on to practice with the quintain in another part of the field. I spent the entire afternoon striving to hook those rings.

My concentration was so taken with attempting to master the skill that I did not notice the passing of time and the emptying of the tiltyard. By mid afternoon, only Goswin was there with me, rehanging each ring when I occasionally managed to spear one. As I tried yet again to spear all the rings along the tilt wall in one pass, I heard the unexpected thunder of hooves racing closer and closer.

I looked up at the last moment to see a helmeted grey knight riding towards me. His lance was only feet away, pointing over the top of the wall and aiming for my body. Without a shield to protect me, I dropped low on Finstar's withers and pulled his head away from the tilt wall to steer us out of danger. Finstar stumbled with the unexpected change of direction. Unseated, I slid from my saddle onto the ground.

The knight rode round the tilt wall and bore down on me before I could do more than get to my feet. His bay horse was cantering wide from the wooden fence I pressed up against. He held his lance in a slacker grip to the left, intending to leave me no option to escape the spear tip but to leap into the path of his horse's hooves. Instead, when he was nearly upon me, I threw myself onto the ground in a tight ball and rolled away along the tilt wall in the direction he had come. This left him no time to adjust his hold. The pointed metal lance tip sliced the air inches above me.

I rolled back onto my feet and ran towards the entrance gate, where Goswin stood holding out a sword and buckler. Once again, the knight rode towards me, leading with his lance. I walked out to meet him half-way between the gate and the tilt wall, brandishing the blunt training sword. When he was only inches away, I stepped onto his wrong side and swivelled round. As I turned, I caught his horse's rein near the bit and pulled it out hard to my right. The horse spun sharply round with me as I stepped back. It nearly fell, and its struggle to keep on its legs brought us both down with it.

The startled knight lay panting on the worn grass. I rolled back onto my feet and went to pull off his helmet to see who he was. Before I could get a firm enough grip, he kicked me in the chest with both feet. I dropped to my knees, winded. He found his feet before I could recover, and ran off past Goswin to escape through the entrance gate.

Chapter 4
An Audience with Oscar

I joined the trainee knights and horsemen in the household cavalry stables where they were tending their horses, helped by the stable hands. While Goswin unsaddled Finstar, I checked over his black coat to make sure he had not been injured in the ambush. Then I chatted with the men who had trained with me, hoping one might have some information about the grey knight.

The young cavalrymen teased me gently about my lack of skill with the lance. They had, however, been impressed by my performances sparring with a sword and handling an axe.

'You played some unusual tricks,' said one. He was a lean blond young man with an energetic manner but a strangely vulnerable look. He reminded me a lot of Rehlein when I had first met the runaway prince. The others called him Klaus.

'The traditional moves you are taught give an excellent grounding, but they are only the start,' I answered him as we strolled together towards the stable door. We walked out into the castle ward.

'Is it true you saw action this summer, Knight Gendal?' he asked.

I nodded. 'That's where I learnt my unusual tricks, in battles and fights like that.'

'How glorious!'

'To you, perhaps. To me, warfare shows a failure of diplomacy. Does your company see much action?'

'Occasional border skirmishes, dealing with bands of robber

brigands, but little else.'

'That is good. It shows a well-run state with effective diplomats. Do all your company wear the Prince's livery? Or do some of you wear their own kit?'

'You are the only knight to train with us without the hart livery.'

We went our separate ways to get ready for the evening meal. I returned to my room deep in thought, wondering who the knight might be who had concealed his identity behind his helmet and grey surcoat. Had someone in the castle not liked my stirring up past secrets about Prince Umbert's death and Sigmund's departure?

I had just finished changing from my training armour to court clothes when a page brought me a summons to join Prince Oscar in the Lesser Hall. I hastened downstairs to do the prince's bidding.

Oscar stood before the empty fireplace in the hall, his right hand supporting his chin as his eyes brooded on a spot on the flagged floor. I could see no difference between the spot he eyed and the rest of the floor, save that it was near the side of the large table where his father had died. I looked up at the ornate tapestries decorating the stone walls around us. The low light coming from the high windows made them hard to see. They appeared to depict scenes from history and fable.

The page announced my presence. Oscar looked up at me, a sad smile on his face. He sat in the chair at the head of the table and beckoned me closer.

'I have had time to consider Sigmund's letter, Knight Gendal. He made certain requests for your benefit. They tell me he held you in great respect.'

I nodded in acknowledgement.

'You know he departed from here under a cloud,' Oscar continued. 'It was in this room he held our father as he died: here, at

27

this table where I sit now.'

I nodded again but stayed silent.

'Lady Herlinde has told me you rescued Sigmund from danger in Strasbourg when he was not able to help himself. You have indeed been his true and faithful friend.'

'Thank you, your Highness.'

'Sigmund's letter asked me to grant you his fiefdom in his memory. He wanted to ensure you no longer need to ride the world in danger for your living. His manor, Rehschloss, stands about half a day's ride from here. It provides a reasonable living from rents and crops, and runs itself. It would be good to have a person with your qualities as a tenant there.'

I bowed low before replying.

'Prince Oscar, your generosity is overwhelming. It is hard for me to disappoint you, but I must decline your offer. I am pledged in service to the Imperator as Ministerialis and Free Knight messenger.'

Oscar gave a wry smile, as if this refusal suited him in some way. Nevertheless, he pressed, 'But that need not prevent you from becoming my vassal, for I too am pledged in service to the Imperator, once a new one is elected.'

'Your Highness, I am a creature of the road. To till the soil and manage serfs is not for me. But one thing I would ask, that you let me shelter here in Harzland through the depths of this winter, once I return from taking the sad news of Prince Sinter's death to his father, Prince Volkmar.'

'You plan to travel on to Schwarzenberg, at this time of year?'

'Yes, your Highness. With your leave, I will go tomorrow morning. The news I have to carry cannot wait any longer.'

I chose not to add that with one attempt to intimidate me only a day after I had arrived, I wanted to make sure the message was delivered before something more serious befell me.

'I see.' Oscar's thoughtful face suggested I had forced him to change plans. 'You are right to want to let my great uncle's family know of Sinter's death. While you are away, I shall instruct Rehschloss to prepare to accommodate you over the winter on your return, for you to use whatever of its resources you require.'

'Thank you, Prince Oscar.'

We walked together to the Great Hall for the evening meal. He signalled for my position at the top table to be improved. At his wish, I took my place between the Chamberlain and Lady Herlinde. The meal again reflected the advent fast, with local fish to supplement the bread and vegetables served by the resourceful kitchen. As the meal progressed, I used my vantage point on the raised top table to watch the crowd, hoping to identify someone of the build and stature of the grey knight. I saw none.

Chapter 5
Journey to Schwarzenberg Castle

I set off from Harzberg soon after dawn the following morning, taking most of my gear with me as a precaution. Before I left, I sent Goswin to Rehschloss with the rest of my possessions and a letter for the castle staff giving guidance about my needs on my return to the Harzland principality.

It was a lovely morning for a long ride, with a light frost, high white clouds in the sky and the gentlest of breezes. My route took me along the main road southeast through the vast forests. There was little traffic as most folks kept to their own hearths at that time of year, but that always increased the risk of danger. I wore my black brigandine and leather helmet over my mail, and my long black cloak for warmth. My sword was in the saddle scabbard and my dagger fastened to my belt. As the journey would take several days, I kept Finstar to a gentle yet steady pace.

This was the sort of time I liked to meditate on the scriptures, the essence of God and the revelation of God's nature in Jesus Christ. But the curious events at Harzberg kept intruding on my thoughts. Why did younger Oscar inherit the crown and not older Sigmund? Who was the person who had disliked me raking up this family disgrace enough to send an unliveried knight to attack me on the training field?

The sound of hoofbeats brought me back to the present. Someone was riding towards me from behind, catching up with me on the road from Harzberg. I turned Finstar and halted in the centre of the road, my hand instinctively on the hilt of my sheathed sword.

The winter-clad knight riding towards me wore the red on white Hart of Harzberg surcoat over his mail, beneath an ample brown cloak which he had wrapped around his arms and legs for warmth. A felted leather helmet protected his head, with padded lappets which covered his ears and shielded the back of his neck. He waved and called out in greeting.

'Knight Gendal! Do not be alarmed. It is I, Knight Klaus,' he called.

'What are you doing here, Klaus?' I asked.

He drew his bay horse to a halt beside me before he answered. The horse was sweating from having been ridden hard. Plumes of condensation blew from its nostrils in the cold air.

'Lady Herlinde sent me to escort you to Schwarzenberg. She

does not want you to fall prey to the brigands who frequent these roads at this time of year.'

The news did not please me. The condition of his horse would delay me on this leg of the journey. However, Herlinde was right, in that two travellers were less likely to be ambushed on the road than one riding alone.

'How considerate of Lady Herlinde,' I replied. 'Are you a member of her retinue?'

He blushed, and I realised why his face had reminded me of Rehlein. I quickly corrected the name in my thoughts to Rehlein's proper name, Sigmund.

'You are also her son?' I asked Klaus.

He shook his head. 'Her cousin. But don't let her know I told you.'

'Don't worry. I am good at keeping secrets. Let's walk on.'

We rode together at an ambling pace until we came to a wayside inn. There we stopped to rest the horses and refresh ourselves. My young companion's conversation was filled with stories of heroes and battles and the search for glory. I let him chatter on, reflecting how far I had come from the days when Rehlein and I had first set out and his conversation had also been filled with the same matters. Once again, I had to remind myself that Rehlein should now be called Prince Sigmund.

Klaus and I set off again early afternoon, as we had a long ride through some of the densest forest before we reached my intended destination for the night, the Bush Inn at Kreuzbruke. It had started to sleet, but the gap between the trees arching over us was so small, the sleet just wetted the centre of the muddy road. The air was still, like the lull before the gathering of a heavy storm.

Shouts shattered the stillness. Four mail-clad men in grey rode out from between the trees and set upon us: two with lances and two wielding axes. I drew my broadsword from my saddle scabbard. Controlling Finstar with my feet rather than his reins, I swung my sword from one side to the other to deflect the lances. One lance leapt up out of the holder's hand; the other impaled the ground with the force of my blow and broke.

I turned to help Klaus, who was fighting axes with his sword and buckler, hampered by his cloak. As Finstar cantered towards his two attackers, they turned and fled, disappearing among the trees. The two lancers followed them into the undergrowth. Their surprise attack having failed, the four vanished as quickly as they had appeared.

The forest returned to its winter stillness. Klaus sat on his bay horse, looking shocked and pale.

'Are you all right?' I asked him.

He nodded. 'I see what you mean, Knight Gendal. The training fields teach only the bare basics of the skills.'

'Your first time in real combat?'

He nodded. 'At least we saw them off.'

'I think not. But I'm certain your presence saved me. They won't be back. Would you like to tell me what is really going on?'

'I overheard someone at the dinner table last night talking about clipping an eagle's wings. As you were the only one at court wearing a surcoat with an eagle, I knew they meant you. I slept on it overnight and asked Lady Herlinde about it this morning. She gave me authority to leave the training and ride as your escort. Except you had long since departed. I rode like the wind to catch up with you.'

'Which then delayed us, letting them catch up with me too as we rested your horse.'

Klaus looked crestfallen to have caused the very thing he had hoped to prevent. I laughed and clapped his shoulder.

'Thanks to you, they have already shot their bolts. I would not expect them to try again. Do you know why they wanted to clip my wings?'

Klaus shook his head, but his expression suggested he knew more than he had said. As we rode on towards Kreuzbruke. I wondered just how trustworthy my new companion really was.

Klaus and I arrived at Schwarzenberg Castle three days later, shortly after the tolling of the noon bell. Schwarzenberg was a rich principality due in good part to the fine wines it produced. Its coat of arms was the full sun on argent, in recognition of the good grape harvest the sun helped ripen on the land's south-facing slopes. The castle stood high on a wooded promontory overlooking the River Briet. The supporting town spread across the slopes about the foot of the promontory. Its thatched timber-framed cottages looked well kept and prosperous. In the streets and market square, friendly people waved at us, recognising Klaus with his Hart surcoat to be a kinsmen and ally of their prince.

Klaus' presence gave us immediate entry to the castle without my having to explain my mission. The guards sent stable hands to tend our horses and a soldier escort to take us to the Great Hall. As we waited there, we admired the hall's plastered and whitewashed walls, a new fashion I had previously come across only in countries further south and east. Soon, our escort returned with an elderly yet vigorous woman wearing a gown of red brocade and green velvet with a matching close-fitting cap to cover her grey hair.

'Pray stand for Lady Ilse,' the soldier announced, though we were already standing.

We bowed towards her.

'Knight Klaus, welcome,' she said with a friendly smile. She turned to look me up and down. 'Who is this you have brought with you?'

'Imperial Knight Gendal, Lady Ilse. We have just ridden from Harzland with bad news,' Klaus replied.

'Yes. I was warned you would.'

Her cryptic reply confused me. Had a messenger reached here before us, or did Lady Ilse practice divination and the dark arts?

She ushered us upstairs to the royal apartments. The soldier followed us and stood on guard outside when we entered the audience chamber and shut the door behind us.

The room was dark and warm, with tapestries across the windows to shut out the winter drafts. My eyes took time to adjust to the low light from the candles burning in two wrought iron stands and the large fire burning in the broad stone hearth.

'My dearest, here are Knight Klaus and Knight Gendal to see you,' Ilse announced, her voice tender.

'Come forward, then, and let me see you,' said Prince Volkmar, his voice abrupt and tired.

He sat close to the crackling fire in a high-backed wooden armchair made comfortable with several cushions. He looked a shell of a man, his once powerful build collapsing in on itself. His lined face was framed with long grey hair and a rough-trimmed beard, and his hands lay thin and bony in his lap.

'How are you keeping, Great Uncle?' Klaus asked.

'Klaus! What a fine young man you're turning out to be! What brings you here?'

'I have come with Knight Gendal. We have brought some bad news for you.'

'Gendal? Gendal - do I know that name? Step forward, Gendal, so that I can see you.'

I did as he bade, and gripped the bony hand that reached out to me, bowing over it as if to give a loyal kiss.

'Gendal was Sigmund's friend,' Klaus prompted.

Volkmar thought awhile and nodded, chuckling. 'Ah, yes, the young guide he went adventuring with. Quite scandalous in its own way: three young men riding off with a woman who wasn't their sister, taking the road to nowhere with their young new guide. Did you find the truth?'

I smiled to hear that question yet again. It must have caused much family debate in the past.

'Not the truth we sought, your Highness. But we did find the truth God wanted for us.'

'It was the making of Sigmund: he went away a moody youth expecting everything to be served him on a plate. He came back a young man who appreciated his princely privileges and understood the lot of others less fortunate. But I'm sure you're not here to reminisce, Gendal. What is your news?'

I hesitated to answer, for I felt a great warmth towards this prickly old man. I drew a deep breath and replied.

'It is with deep regret I have to inform you that your son Prince Sinter died in battle at the end of September. He perished with Prince Sigmund at Dernfels, fighting beside Count Bertram of Rabenberg against Nicolaus, Duke of Danuvia.'

'Sinter? Sigmund? Dead?' He laughed in denial. 'Oh, no - they are just in the next room.'

His response dismayed but did not surprise me. Sinter had been quite dismissive about his father's mental acuity in the past.

'No, your Highness: they are dead,' I replied with compassion.

'Nonsense. They are just in the next room.'

'Please forgive me, your Highness: I am struggling to

understand. Do you mean metaphysically, as in they have gone before us to meet our Maker and theirs?'

'Not at all. Physically. Go and look.'

He pointed towards the door. His reaction disappointed me. I had hoped he would be able to provide me with the answers to a lot of questions which members of the Hirschmann family had avoided. But when his grasp of reality was so poor, how could I trust anything he said? He saw my expression and gave a short, wry chuckle.

'You've got something more on your mind, Knight Gendal, haven't you! Out with it.'

I dared not tell him my true thoughts, but recalled one of Sinter's comments and fell back on asking about that.

'Thank you for your perceptiveness, your Highness. Prince Sinter told us once he had joined Count Bertram against Duke Nicolaus and Condottiero Maladriuzzi, because he had a bone to pick with one about reneging on a contract and the other for killing his best hound. Was that true?'

'Of course not! When Sigmund came begging for money for the Count, I sent Sinter and a few men along with the gold, to keep him safe. Sigmund had been badly wronged in Harzland, and I wasn't going to let him throw his life away for no good reason.'

A thrill of excitement shot through my body at this unexpected revelation.

'Alas, your Highness. I should have left Sigmund drinking himself to death at the Bush Inn in Strasbourg, instead of making him rush headlong into someone else's fight. He would have lived longer.'

'Ah, but that would not have been living. Sigmund always saw himself as a hero of old. Hard drinking and fighting heroic battles are all a part of that.'

'Why didn't Sigmund succeed his father? Why was Oscar crowned instead?'

The old prince gave another of those canny wry smiles.

'Are you asking me to betray family secrets, messenger?'

'No, your Highness. I am trying to understand why the traditional line of succession was ignored: firstborn son to firstborn son.'

He sat silently for a while, his chin in his left hand as he considered how to answer me.

'Sigmund was holding his father in his arms when he died. Umbert demanded a drink. Sigmund put the goblet to his lips. When Umbert drank, he choked to death. Oscar and his mother Herlinde accused Sigmund of poisoning him.'

I looked at Klaus. 'Did you see that?'

Klaus shook his head. 'I was still with the Maying party. We were late for the meal after the Castellan gave us a lecture. We had not tended our horses before seeing to ourselves. When we finally took our places at table, two seats were empty: Sigmund's and his father's; and we all ate in silence.'

The chamber also fell silent as we all thought about this. The only sounds came from the crackling logs burning in the fire.

'Your Highness, may I test your patience further, with another question?' I asked.

Volkmar chuckled. 'I don't mind you testing my patience at all, Gendal. It is a pleasure to talk to someone other than the servants and these four walls.'

Ilse drew in a sharp intake of breath at his unthinking comment. I felt for her, guessing that the long hours she spent supporting her husband did not count in his eyes.

'Your Highness, five hundred gold coins was a vast sum to loan someone in Sigmund's situation. Why did you agree to give him the money?'

'A curious question, Gendal,' Volkmar replied. 'I knew he could repay me.'

'And were you repaid?'

He raised an eyebrow, warning that I was treading on thinner ground.

'Of course. I sent his promissory note to Rehschloss, and his household returned the sum within a fortnight. It was not the first time they had made such payments, to others though, not to me. Why did you think to ask that?'

'It tells me your relationship with Sigmund was every bit as close and trusting as he had led me to believe. Even though he had been accused of murdering your nephew, by your niece in law and your great nephew.'

'As I said, Sigmund had been badly wronged in Harzland. I am just sorry I cannot tell you more. Like Klaus, I was elsewhere when Prince Umbert died. So go ask your questions somewhere else.'

I bowed and withdrew, leaving Prince Volkmar to talk alone with Klaus under Ilse's watchful eye.

Chapter 6
Return to Harzland

Klaus and I returned to Harzland within the week. Klaus made a pleasant companion on the road, and the distances passed more quickly with his conversation. We arrived back at Harzberg on the 12th of December, and rode directly to the castle to inform Prince

Oscar of our return to his principality.

We entered the castle at dusk, having hurried the last stage of our journey because the moon was new, making night travel difficult. The town gates were closing as we approached, but the gateman saw Klaus' surcoat with the Hart device of the household cavalry and let us through, shutting the gate behind us as the last travellers entering the town that day.

We rode on through the shadowy streets up the hill towards the castle and found those gates also shut. Klaus knocked on the doors with a coded rap used by the cavalry.

'Who's that trying to get in after dusk? Can't you see the gates are closed?' complained the keeper.

'Knight Gendal and Knight Klaus, just arrived from Schwarzenberg,' I called back.

'Knight Klaus, can you vouch for Gendal?'

'Yes, Johan,' Klaus called back: 'Knight Klaus vouches for Knight Gendal.'

Convinced by the use of his name and the sound of Klaus's voice, the gatekeeper opened one of the massive gates to admit us, muttering all the time. I presumed his resentment arose from our late arrival giving him more work.

Klaus called his squire from the barracks to tend to our horses and instructed his page to let Prince Oscar know we had arrived safely back from Schwarzenberg. Though we waited in the Great Hall to be received by the prince, he did not trouble to see for himself that we had returned. Instead, he sent the Chamberlain to confirm the prince knew of our presence in the castle.

Before I had left Schwarzenberg, Prince Volkmar had given me a sealed letter to take to Oscar, with the instruction to give it to him in person when I saw him next, At the time, I had not understood why he had cautioned me not to mention the letter or insist on seeing Oscar to deliver it. It now appeared that Volkmar had some idea of how my return would be received.

At the evening meal, the Chamberlain demoted me to eating with the household cavalry. This was not a hardship as I enjoyed their banter and tall tales. Klaus entertained his colleagues with an embellished version of our travelling adventures. Occasionally, I looked up at the people on the top table on the dais. They avoided letting my gaze catch their eyes. Oscar appeared to pay a lot of heed to his uncle Heinrich, who in turn listened a lot to two well-dressed men also seated along from them. When I asked Klaus about these, he told me they were Lord Arnulf and Sheriff Opecz. Throughout the meal, Herlinde kept her head low as if she had disagreed with the situation.

I grateful not to have left any of my possessions at the castle earlier because it meant I did not have to seek permission to return to my previous room in the Royal apartments to retrieve them. That night, the cavalrymen happily found me a bed in the barracks. I slept well enough and rose with them at the crack of dawn to prepare our horses for the early morning exercise ride.

The company of cavalrymen lined up in the courtyard and rode out in pairs through the main gate. Klaus paired with me and placed us in the middle of the formation.

'That will make it harder for the gatekeeper to stop you leaving,' he said, knowing it would mean stopping half the cavalry to turn me back.

'Why? Are they trying to keep me here?' I asked.

He did not reply, making me wonder once again whether he was friend or foe.

Our company rode off through the streets and out of the city in a column of twos on their routine daily circuit. Out in the forest, the column followed broad, well-trodden tracks between the evergreen and deciduous trees. We left the river behind and travelled through the hinterland hills.

After a good hour's ride, we descended towards the river again.

'When the river comes into view, take the next turning left,' Klaus warned me. 'The rest of us will ride on down the hill. The lane will take you to the main road north. Turn left again and the road will take you towards Rehberg.'

'What have you heard, Klaus? Why are you helping me this way?'

'That's what Sigmund would have wanted.'

'Do you know why they have changed towards me?'

Before he could answer, we rounded a bend and the river came into view. The lane lay immediately after that. I pressed with my right leg to turn Finstar left down the narrow grassy track, and left the formation without the other knights having to change pace.

The green lane headed down the forested hill more gently than the track we had left. It eventually came out on the riverbank road. I turned left again as instructed and easily found my way to Rehschloss Castle, arriving soon after the noon bell had tolled.

Sigmund's castle was a welcoming old pile of a rugged building, topping a high craggy tor above the river. When I turned off the village main street and took the road up to the castle, the villagers watched me with friendly interest as they went about their work.

The castle gates stood open for my arrival. Goswin ran out of the kitchens to welcome me in the cobbled courtyard. I dismounted and asked him to show me to the stables.

'The servants will want to meet you first,' he warned.

As he spoke, the people who ran the castle rushed out of various doorways and lined up on the steps of the Great Hall to welcome me. I handed Finstar's reins to Goswin and turned aside to meet them all. Their friendly respect was refreshing after the hostile reception I had experienced at Oscar's court.

Once the Steward Dietl had introduced me to all the servants he took me to his office. This room stood next to the Great Hall and had just the one door which opened onto the courtyard. Several dark wood cupboards lined the walls, and a low fire burned in the small hearth, keeping the place warm.

Dietl was a tall, lean man with a well-worn face behind the bushy dark brown hair and beard. With calloused hands used to hard work, he brought out the estate documents to show me. Then realising I might be hungry after my journey, he moved a tabby cat off a chair for me to sit and offered me refreshments.

'Some bread and cheese, and a herb tea; perhaps mint if your kitchen has any,' I requested.

'It is your kitchen now, Knight Gendal,' he replied, smiling with approval at my simple choices. I wondered if his late master Sigmund had drunk heavily long before he left on the path that took him to the Bush Inn at Strasbourg.

'Dietl, I have little experience of fiefs and estates. All my adult life I have been a traveller. For the short time I plan to stay here, I shall rely on you to continue running this estate as you have done in the past for Sigmund.'

'I thank you for your confidence in me, Knight Gendal. It would be an honour to escort you around your new estate this afternoon.'

'I would rather do that tomorrow morning - I have done a lot of riding of late. And I would like to explore this homely old castle first: this humble place Rehlein called home.'

Dietl looked up at me in surprise. 'How do you know that

name?'

'It was the name Sigmund chose to use when he rode with me. Some travellers like to use an alias, to protect their identity on the road. Where does it come from?'

'It was his mother's cradle name for him: my little deer. He must have trusted you implicitly.'

I turned aside, remembering Sigmund standing in his surcoat and mail in the sunlight at the Wolfholz Tavern, a golden prince among men only days before his death. A stray tear trickled from my right eye.

Dietl nodded in recognition. 'We miss him too. You are among friends here.'

The castle proved to be everything I liked in an old home: unpretentious and cared for without show. Its library was sparse, its armoury and trophy rooms well-stocked. After the tour ended, I returned to the library to look at the few books on its shelves. Heroic tales, fables and romances outnumbered the religious works.

'What do you think of our little collection, Knight Gendal?' asked a voice from behind me.

I spun round to face an elderly man in black robes and a four-pointed hat, standing in the doorway. Age had shortened him, and his lined face was creased further by a friendly smile.

'Welcome, Knight Gendal. I am Dr Petrus. I was Prince Sigmund's tutor, in the days when he was still called Rehlein.'

'He used Rehlein as his travelling name, too. It would have kept him safe from kidnappers. He was a credit to your teaching, Dr Petrus.'

'I taught him for many years. He loved to read about heroes, especially his namesake Sigmund. We spent hours studying their exploits: David, Alexander, Jason, Agamemnon, Arthur, Beowulf, and so many more.'

Petrus sat at a well-used oak table and gestured to me to sit opposite him. We felt quite at ease in each other's company, even though we had not met before. I moved a tabby cat off the seat and took its place.

'Sigmund died a hero's death, fighting for justice and freedom,' I said.

'He would have accepted that, as a good death, a heroic death. He had wanted to be a hero from the age of seven. When he was ten, he realised all true heroes went on a quest before they could be called heroes. When he disappeared just before his eighteenth birthday, I realised he had left to follow his quest.'

'Did he not discuss it with you beforehand?'

I looked at the old tutor. He gave an enigmatic smile.

'Yes, he did. But I never told his family. They didn't think to ask me.'

'What happened?'

'He came back from drinking in one of the local taverns; so excited. His eyes shone, and he looked alive in a way I had not seen before.'

I remembered that look, and the young blond knight who had sat drinking with me in a bar, his eyes glowing as he questioned me about my quest to find the truth.

'What did he say?'

'He told me he had met an amazing traveller, a member of the Worshipful Company of Guides and Messengers, who had gathered two companions to go seeking after truth. One was a poet, and one was an independent young woman who dressed like a man. And their guide, I believe, was you.'

'It was. What did you advise him?'

'The next night, I went to the tavern with him to observe the three of you together. I saw that you were headstrong and idealistic, but basically honourable, and you had no regard for his class and station in life. I had already come to the end of what I could teach him. A few months spent on the road following such a naïve quest would give him the greatest experience. So I told him to go.'

I nodded. 'And so he became the third of the Four. A merchant's son joined us a couple of weeks later. Then off we went, searching for truth.'

'Where did you take them?'

'We went to Italy first, and then to Greece. We visited the Franciscans, and the followers of Hildegard, and countless other places. None of them had the answers we didn't know we needed.'

'How did your quest end?'

'We were doubling back across the Holy Roman Empire towards France. One by one, each of the Four left our search for truth and returned to their fantasies. And I found myself in Sluthe Wood, where I received my life's commission: to seek justice for the poor, to defend the oppressed, and set the captive free. It taught me, some things one can only do alone.'

'Yes, that can be true; but for a commission like yours, surely you do need other people to help and support you.'

'Isaiah was a voice crying in the wilderness, and we still read that prophet's words.'

'As did our Lord Jesus Christ, and he had many followers.'

'But all except a few women left Him at the end. So I came to understand it was right for Sigmund and the others to leave me and go back to their former stations.'

'Sigmund came back to us a changed man after his time with you. You had taught him well: how to live without power and influence and wealth, to be loyal to your companions and to be grateful for small mercies. You had also taught him respect for all people, no matter what their status or position in life, and the importance of prudence, dependability, and compassion.'

'Those things I didn't teach him: he developed them himself.'

'You taught him the best way, through living it. He learned the truth of most people's experiences, how life and mother nature are hard on those who are poor. And how the poor are obliged to work to keep dukes and princes in the luxury they desire. He would have made a very good Crown Prince.'

Petrus paused in reflection, wondering whether to raise his next point. He took courage and ventured it.

'It is a pity you have chosen not to take on our estate as fief. It is not too late to change your mind.'

'Foxes have holes and birds have nests, but the Son of Man has nowhere to lay his head,' I said.

'Are you claiming to be like our Lord Jesus Christ?'

'Of course not. But as the learned Thomas Aquinas wrote, the imitation of Christ is the path to religious perfection.'

'You are acquainted with such writings?'

'I studied a little at Toulouse at the Imperator's behest: the Dominican establishment seeking canonisation for this learned member of theirs.'

'Was that before or after your youthful search for truth?'

'Some time after. Once I gave up self-pity, God was able to transform my career.'

'You are a good person. Perhaps we can prevail upon you to change your mind?'

'While there is life and breath, there is always the chance to change one's mind.'

Chapter 7
An Unexpected Invitation

During my first evening meal at Rehschloss, I tried to sit with the servants in the Great Hall as I wanted to hear their memories of Sigmund. Steward Dietl would not hear of it, and Dr Petrus agreed with him. They sat on either side of me at the table on the dais, giving me an honour I did not consider my due.

The food was good: venison from the forest, vegetables from the village gardens, fruit from the castle orchards, and golden bread baked from the wheat flour ground by the river mills. Many drank the local wine, but I chose to drink the water from the castle well.

Knowing that most of the staff would rise early the next morning to carry out their duties, I retired to my room soon after the meal was over. I left the stone-built hall and took the spiral staircase to the timber-framed apartments above. It was a relief to be alone at last after the long day. I sank into the welcoming warmth of the canopied feather bed in what had been Sigmund's private chamber.

The room was simply furnished with a wooden press, a table and chair, and a stand for a ewer and basin near the bed. The counterpane had been woven from undyed wool, and a cured deer hide lay as a rug beside the bed. Internal shutters covered the two windows overlooking the castle courtyard. The appearance of the room put me in mind of a hunting lodge rather than a home. It lacked the tender touches a wife might have added to the furnishings.

I fell asleep quickly, my consciousness snuffed out like a candle. It had been many days since I had been able to relax and sleep soundly in safe surroundings.

Strange noises disturbed my sleep some time later in the middle of the night. I struggled back into awareness, hearing scuffles in the wall behind the bedhead. Deciding that it must have been a rat or mouse in the wainscot, I soon fell back to sleep again.

Goswin woke me in the morning with a knock at the door. He carried in a breakfast tray of cheese, bread, and mint tea. When he opened the shutters, the cold grey light of another icy winter day cast its silver frosting over the room. Finding frozen water in the ewer, I dressed in my warmest clothes for the day's main task: the ride with Dietl to inspect the estate.

Dr Petrus joined us, to my surprise and pleasure, for I found him an amiable companion. His reason became clear as Dietl took us on a tour of the fief. They showed me abundant hunting forests, well-tended vineyards, fertile farmlands, industrious vassals and healthy livestock, hoping to persuade me that the fief could run itself should I change my mind and accept the bequest.

The sun was sinking behind the hills when we rode back up to the castle. As we trotted through the gateway into the courtyard, Goswin came out to meet us with Knight Klaus beside him and another of Oscar's men-at-arms behind.

'Klaus! What brings you here?' I asked in welcome.

I leapt down from Finstar and handed his reins to Goswin to take him to the stables.

'Prince Oscar sent me to deliver this letter to you,' Klaus replied.

I nodded my thanks to Dietl and Petrus to dismiss them, and walked with Klaus into the Great Hall.

'Have you eaten, Klaus? Do you need food and drink?' I asked.

'Yes, Gendal, we have eaten. Your servants have been very hospitable. We arrived soon after noon.'

I looked around for his escort but could not see him and assumed he had gone back to the stables with Goswin.

We sat down at the top table. Klaus handed me a letter sealed with the Hart of Harzland wax-stamp.

'Do you know what this is about?' I asked as I broke the seal to open the letter.

'I think Prince Oscar was persuaded to listen to Lady Herlinde rather than Lord Heinrich. I am to take your response by return.'

The letter ran: *To the Ministerialis Knight Gendal, Prince Oscar greets you. You are invited to join the Royal Household for our Winter Boar Hunt and Solstice Ball a week hence.*

Oscar had written below the scribe's neat script in his own untidy hand, *We were disappointed that you felt the need to leave Harzberg for Rehschloss so soon;* and had signed the letter himself.

I dropped the letter on the table in dismay.

'Does he really mean this?'

Klaus picked up the letter and read it slowly, his reading skills not being his strongest point. When he put it down again, he looked at me with eyebrows furrowed in bewilderment.

'If the Prince didn't mean it, I am sure he wouldn't have written this to invite you. Do you not want to go? It is a splendid affair.'

'The last ball I attended, someone abducted me at knifepoint and tried to have me murdered. Is the Solstice Ball a regular event?'

Klaus nodded. 'The Winter Hunt and Solstice Ball are both traditions of the Hirschmann household. We celebrate the end of the sun's old year and the coming of the new. It is very popular. Everyone who is anyone in Harzland attends.'

'A pagan celebration in Advent?'

'A farming festival, I was brought up to believe. Without the sun, we would have no harvest, from which our wealth comes. Most guests stay on for the later celebration on Christmas Eve and depart again on Christmas Day.'

The thought of staying at Harzberg from the 20th to the 25th of December filled me with apprehension after my last visit to the castle, but convention required me to attend.

'Because I stay here on Prince Oscar's sufferance, Klaus, I cannot refuse his invitation, though I dearly wish I could. Bear with me, while I go to write a response.'

I left Klaus in the Great Hall and went to the library to find some paper and a pen to compose a reply. Petrus was sitting at the table by the library window when I entered. He had opened some books for guidance as he drew a heraldic device on a fresh sheet of paper using inks and a quill pen he had made himself.

'Gendal, you look concerned.'

'Some of your paper, if I may, good doctor. I have to write a response to a letter from Prince Oscar.'

He retrieved a sheet of paper from a folder kept on one of the bookshelves, moved a tabby cat from the spare seat by the table for me, and let me use his own pen and ink. I was aware of him looking casually at the contents of my letter as I wrote:

To the most esteemed Prince Oscar of Harzland, your guest Knight Gendal humbly greets you from Rehschloss. Your invitation is cordially accepted in the spirit it was sent. I look forward to enjoying your hospitality at Harzberg for the Winter Solstice Hunt and Ball, and shall join your goodly company from the evening of 20th December. May God keep you safe and grant you a long reign.
I signed the letter with a flourish, blotted it with a little sand, folded it carefully and sealed it with the mark of my Imperial Ministerialis ring.

'You are honoured, Knight Gendal,' Petrus remarked. 'This is a great family event. Most of the Hirschmann family will be there, and even the Schwarzenbergs. And there will be plenty of opportunities to impress the ladies.'

'You won't get me to marry and settle down that easily, Petrus,' I said with a smile.

I returned to the Great Hall and handed Klaus my letter of acceptance.

'Would you like to stay here for the night, before you return to Harzberg?' I asked him.

Klaus smiled but shook his head.

'Unfortunately, my instructions were to return as soon as you gave me your reply. Will we have the pleasure of your company at the hunt?'

'Of course. But may I prevail upon you to stay until at least tomorrow morning? The sun has set, and the moon has not yet reached its first quarter, so your ride will not be easy. We could spend time over dinner to discuss what happened during my last visit to Harzberg.'

'Alas, I must return straightway. I have other invitations to take out this week, too. As for your last visit to Harzberg, I have been informed your reception was due to an oversight.'

His response drew a cynical laugh from me before I could censure it. I clapped his shoulder and replied, 'I am glad to hear that, Klaus, but sorry to see you go. Have a safe journey back.'

He gave me a short courtesy bow and left to take my answer back to Oscar. As he withdrew from the Great Hall, Petrus wandered in as though he had just been passing.

'What oversight happened in Harzberg?' he enquired, looking at me with a penetrating stare of concern, like a wise and knowledgeable owl. He must have been a formidable teacher to the young princes in their earlier days.

'It was nothing. I was made less welcome on my second arrival than I had been on my first. People often like to blame the messenger for the message.'

His impatient snort told me he knew I had fobbed him off and would not let the matter rest that way for long.

Chapter 8
The Ghost of Rehschloss

Once again I fell asleep swiftly that night, but not for long. A crash close by startled me awake from a deep sleep at some time in the middle of the night. The clatter sounded as if it had come from somewhere in my chamber. I lay still in bed, my ears straining to hear any further noise to indicate the danger.

After years of travelling in wild places, my hearing is very good. But not even a surreptitious intake of breath disturbed the night's stillness. I wondered why no-one else had reacted to the crash. Then I recalled most of the castle's inhabitants lived in the servants' quarters in another part of the castle. Only Dietl and Petrus had rooms in the royal apartments, somewhere near the stone spiral staircase further away down the corridor.

In one of Sigmund's last private conversations with me just four days before he died in battle, he had referred to his castle as he gave me his ring and letter to take to his brother Oscar in the event of his death: *Fear not: they shall welcome you honourably in my name. They may even offer you my castle as fief for your trouble – no-one in my family likes its non-existent ghosts.*

During my travels, I had come across many tales of ghosts and haunted places. Like Sigmund, I believed there were usually more mundane causes for such events than disturbed spirits. However, in the depth of night in a strange room, it was all too easy to give credence to the spirits and doubt Sigmund's confidence. I prayed for divine protection and eventually fell back into a fitful, broken sleep.

Goswin woke me again the next day with a breakfast tray of bread and cheese. When I stirred, he opened the shutters to let in the light. I saw that the room was in good order, just as I had left it when I got into bed. Wherever the crash had come from, it had not been in my bedroom.

'Goswin, does anyone use the rooms on either side of this?' I asked.

He shook his head. 'No, Sir. Steward Dietl and Dr Petrus have the rooms closest to the stairs. The Lady's Chamber between you and them is not used. Will you be riding out today?'

'Perhaps, after lunch. This morning, after you have tended to Finstar, spend some time in the kitchens. Offer to help the cooks and ask them to tell you all the folk tales they have heard about this castle.'

The page looked crestfallen. I realised he took my request to be a demotion and smiled to reassure him.

'They are far more likely to tell you the old tales than they would me, Goswin: the gorier, the better.'

He nodded in deference to my authority and left to carry out my instructions.

Once I had dressed and breakfasted, I went to look at the rooms on either side of mine. The Lady's Chamber was furnished in a similar fashion but with more feminine touches in the choices of materials: rose damask counterpane and drapes, and a lighter stain on the oak furniture. The other room was a guest chamber, fitted out with the best of ornately carved furniture, green damask furnishings and hunting tapestries on the walls. This would be the room where Oscar stayed whenever he visited Rehschloss. Neither room showed a sign that anything was amiss. Nothing was present that could have caused the crash in the night.

I went to the library, wondering where else to search. Dr Petrus was at his favourite table, poring over the old books again. He welcomed me and invited me to join him there. I took the seat opposite him, the place where I had sat to write the letter the evening before.

'Did anything wake you in the middle of the night, Petrus?' I asked.

'No? Why, did something wake you?' he asked. His face looked guileless: I did not doubt that his reply was genuine.

'There was quite a crash, during in the night. It sounded as if something had fallen in my room. But when I awoke this morning, nothing was out of place.'

'These lath and plaster walls are quite thin. Perhaps you heard a rat in the wainscot in your sleep and your dreams made it much bigger.'

'Perhaps. But it must have been a very large rat indeed to make such a din. So this castle has no stories of ghostly happenings?'

Petrus smiled like a kindly teacher indulging his imaginative pupil.

'The only ghosts in this place are memories,' he replied. His smile became wistful. 'We all miss Prince Sigmund. None of us believed he had committed the crime of which he was accused.'

'What crime was that?' I encouraged.

'His father choked to death in his arms. Those who saw them

first accused Sigmund of poisoning Umbert.'

Petrus' statement helped me make more sense of other people's remarks about Umbert's death. Their comments fell into one of two opposing sides. People who had supported Sigmund spoke of an injustice. Those who had accused Sigmund were glad to hear he had died an honourable death and would trouble the family no more.

'How did they plan to prosecute Sigmund?' I asked.

'There was talk of trial by combat by Sheriff Opecz, but they decided against that. Everyone knew Sigmund was more skilled on the field than Oscar. Heinrich suggested they drag him off to the court of Louis, the self-styled King of Rome, to be judged by his Lord and his Peers. Sigmund vanished the next day.'

'And he ended up at the Bush Inn in Strasbourg, where I stumbled across him again. Were you present at Harzberg when Prince Umbert died?'

'Sadly, no. Dietl and I do not move in those exalted circles. The May Day hunt and ball were an opportunity for Umbert and Herlinde to find Sigmund and Oscar suitable wives.'

'Did Sigmund want to wed?'

'Ah. Now, thereby hangs a tale.' Petrus smiled and thought through his next comments before voicing them. 'All the ladies had eyes only for Sigmund. They thought him brave, dashing and heroic; and he did look the hero he had always aspired to be. He had an excellent physique and was fair of form and face. His younger brother Oscar was eclipsed in his presence, a pale imitation of him, like the moon's light against the sun's.'

I nodded in understanding, recalling my first opinion of Oscar, having known Sigmund.

Petrus continued, 'Sigmund was also clearer in his thinking and confident in his decisions, like his father. Oscar was more like his mother Herlinde, and equally as influenced by her brother Heinrich.'

'His uncle?'

Petrus nodded. 'Harzberg Castle is a changed place since Heinrich became the puppet master.'

'So the frosty reception I received when I returned there last Wednesday was Heinrich's doing?'

'And Klaus is related to him.'

I sat back in dismay as more pieces of the puzzle fell into place. Klaus had befriended me with ulterior motives. Though he had helped me escape the castle, he had deliberately delayed me on the road to Schwarzenberg to give the four knights the chance to catch me up and warn me off.

'Where did Klaus spend yesterday afternoon?' I asked, dry-mouthed.

Although my question was hypothetical, Petrus gave me a literal response.

'You would need to ask elsewhere. I was out with you and Dietl when Klaus and his squire arrived.'

I thanked the doctor and left him to his books in the library, thinking the castle servants might have the answer to that question. As I crossed the courtyard towards the stables, Goswin left the kitchens and joined me.

'Have you found out anything for me, Goswin?' I asked.

'Yes, sir.'

We both turned our backs to the chill wind that was blowing about the yard. I looked back at the building which housed the two halls and the royal apartments. For the first time, I noticed that there were three storeys to the structure: the stone-walled halls on the ground floor, the half-timber royal apartments above, and the timber-framed attic floor below the tiled roof.

I ushered Goswin out of the wind into the Lesser Hall and sat down at the worn fireside table to hear his report.

'The cook wanted to send me packing, but the kitchen maid was glad of my help. I fetched her fuel and water. She said the castle used to be plagued with rats and mice. The Steward got some good mousing cats from the village, and after that they didn't hear any more stories of ghosts.'

I smiled, recalling both Dietl and Petrus moving cats from chairs to let me sit.

'Did they tell you anything about the history of this castle?'

'It was built hundreds of years ago by Prince Sigmund's ancestor Lothar. A dragon used to terrorise the villagers. It burnt the crops with its fiery breath and ate the children. It used to perch on the crag where this castle stands now. From there, it watched the river and chose its prey. Lothar put on a cloak which hid him in the trees. He crept up on the dragon. When he got very close, he drew his sword. The blade scraped the scabbard as it came out. The noise made the dragon turn. It tried to breathe fire on Lothar, but he was too close. He stabbed the dragon in its vent and slid his sword upwards against the scales, killing it. Then he built his castle here to stop any more dragons coming to use the crag as a perch.'

'That's a good story, Goswin. Alas, it doesn't help us today. But there is one place we haven't searched yet: upstairs, on the top floor.'

We went next door to the Great Hall and took the stone spiral staircase past the royal apartments to the third storey. This would have housed the children's rooms in earlier days. Though the passage was clean, the sparsely furnished rooms behind each door were dusty and neglected, and very cold. The wooden floors were made of smooth plain planks, marked and dented in places by previous occupants long since gone.

I opened the shutters in one of the rooms to see where I was standing in relation to my bedroom on the floor below. The view showed me the next room to my left was the one directly above where I had slept.

I ran into the room, threw open the shutters, and looked around. A cascade of household items and metal implements lay scattered across the wooden floor in a large puddle of water. Nothing else was in the room.

Goswin sprang forward to lift up a pewter trencher.

'Cook was looking for this! It went missing last night!'

'So that's what Klaus and his friend were doing yesterday afternoon!'

I looked through all the scattered items, trying to work out how Klaus had managed to pile them up in such a way that they would fall during the night, long after his departure.

Two of the bigger utensils were wet inside: a large copper brewing funnel and a broad brass pan. All the other items were dry or just splashed or sitting in the puddle on the floor.

'Goswin, go and tell Dr Petrus what we have found. He will be in the library. Ask him to come up here and see this. Then take the trencher to the Cook and ask her to send some of the kitchen hands up here to return all these items to their proper places.'

Goswin nodded and rushed off at once.

I went to the window and looked out at the courtyard. After a few moments, Goswin appeared below me and raced across to the kitchen. Behind me, the door creaked open and Petrus walked in. I turned to watch him as he inspected the pile of equipment scattered across the floor.

'I see you have found your ghost, Gendal,' he said with a wry smile.

'It was right above my head where I slept,' I replied. 'No wonder Klaus did not want to stay the night. But how did he get this pile to fall long after he was safely back at Harzberg?'

Petrus laughed. 'You clearly haven't been a teacher. Let me give you a clue. This could not have happened in summer.'

I tried hard to find the answer to his riddle but failed. My head was so filled with thoughts of anger and betrayal that I could not think clearly.

'No, you will need to explain it to me, Doctor.'

'Whoever did build this tower of metal objects; bearing in mind it might not have been Klaus, though I understand you jumping to that conclusion. Yes, whoever built it balanced the brewing funnel above the brass pan, with the pan angled slightly away. He filled the brewing funnel with ice. When the fire was lit in your room, it warmed this room a little too, and the ice started to melt. The water dripped into the pan. Every drip made the pile more unsteady. When the last drip took the balance over the tipping point, the whole pile toppled and crashed to the floor.'

'And I awoke, fearing a foe was about to attack me in my sleep!'

Chapter 9
The Book of Heraldry

I spent the next day relaxing in the library at Rehschloss with Dr Petrus. The people who served us and kept the castle running seemed somehow more kindly disposed towards me after the unmasking of the ghost. They felt relieved that none of their number had turned out to be a pilferer. They were also glad that all the castle's missing items had turned up again, after being used by our brief visitors in a failed attempt to scare me.

While Petrus worked at his desk in the better light by the window, I sat near the fire with a cat on my lap and a beautifully illuminated copy of the New Testament open upon a rotating lectern. It was a pleasant way to spend a winter afternoon.

'Dr Petrus, I do love this old castle, and the peace sitting in this library with you. It somehow makes me feel closer to Sigmund, even though I know he would not have spent much time here himself.'

'That is true. Rehlein was never one for study, though he loved reading about the heroes of old. That is how I tempted him to learn to read.'

'What did you think of his cousin Sinter's influence over him?'

'Ah. Prince Sinter was very quick-witted, and a little too self-confident. He tended to dazzle Rehlein.'

'He tended to make Rehlein far more flippant and self-centred. I could always tell when he had been with him.'

Petrus smiled indulgently. 'Rehlein delighted in drinking from Sinter's cup. He loved him, you know, the way the outlawed David loved King Saul's son Jonathan. But unlike Jonathan and David, I am not sure that that deep regard was returned.'

Surprised by Petrus' reference, I exchanged the New Testament for a codex containing the books of Samuel, and read through that part of David's story in its elegant Latin script to remind myself of the reference.

A commotion in the courtyard below the library drew us over to the window. We watched for a few moments as some kitchen hands chased after a hen which had escaped from their clutches. When I turned back from the window, I noticed the papers scattered across the doctor's desk. The uppermost sheet showed a precise depiction of the heraldic device of two crossed cleaver falchions in gold on a vert field. Below the illustration had been penned the name Arnulf Althaus.

Petrus joined me at the desk and moved the top sheet to show others, including a drawing of the device of two parallel wavy blue lines on argent.

'This is my conceit, Gendal: to write a compendium of heraldic devices in use in the Holy Roman Empire these days. Rehschloss provides me with an abundance of materials to make the paints and ink, and the monastery near Harzberg is happy to sell me whatever cannot be made here.'

'How interesting. I did serve briefly as one of the Imperator's heralds. Such a book would have been very useful for me. Is that the true badge of Lord Arnulf?'

'Yes. And this other is the true badge of Lord Opecz.'

'Then why do they not wear them?'

'More to the point, Gendal, why do they now reside at Harzberg and not where their ancestral homelands lie?'

'Are you able to answer that for me?'

He looked at me with merry eyes and a crooked smile.

'Now, that I can't tell you, but not because I want to vex you. All I know is that one spring, quite a few years ago now, three waves of refugees came across the bridge by Harzberg. Some time later that same year, Lord Opecz and Lord Arnulf ingratiated themselves into Prince Umbert's court. The prince was feeling some of the infirmities from a hard life and was glad to have two vigorous and decisive younger men to support him, when one of his sons eschewed weapons and the other was always off elsewhere looking for battles to fight.'

'Fie on you, Petrus! For leading me to the brink and abandoning me there.'

He laughed. 'Ah, but you can go and find out. Their ancestral lands were fiefs granted their forebears by the Dukes of Romfeld. Duke Albrecht's seat is but two days' journey through the forests on the far side of the river. While he may not give you an audience, I am sure your skills will help you happen upon someone else who can give you the answers you seek.'

'How do you know me so well after so little time?'

'You forget, we first met when you were the young messenger who lured Rehlein and others to join you in your search for truth. That was many years ago, long before Lord Arnulf and Lord Opecz turned up in Harzberg.'

And so the next morning, I crossed the river by the local cable ferry and rode through the forested hills into the lands of the Duchy of Romfeld. The journey was unexceptional, but blighted by milder days of heavy rain. It was a relief to find the shelter of a roadside hostelry to dry my clothes, rub down Finstar, and find food to eat.

The evening of the second day brought me to the city of Wohlstadt, the seat of the Duke of Romfeld, where I was one of the last to be admitted inside the city walls before sunset. I found an agreeable inn to stay in overnight, which could even provide me with a separate room. As my wet clothes steamed dry in front of the fire in my bedroom, I dressed casually in shirt and breeches and joined the other travellers in the public bar. I ordered dumpling stew from a choice of three dishes on the tavern menu.

The inn had few staying guests, but the bar was busy with local merchants socialising after a day of strong sales. After I had eaten, I took the risk of offering to buy a round of drinks for a group of three mercers who stood apart from the rest. They dressed well in costly velvet coats and breeches, one brown, one deep blue and one an earthy green; and wore expensive polished leather footwear of a style that was more than a shoe but less than a boot. They happily accepted my invitation and sat down at my table to talk about themselves and ask about my own business.

I revealed my Guild of Guides and Messengers badge.

'I have been sent here to find Lord Opecz, who I was told had a fief in this Duchy,' I said.

The mercers looked at each other with frowning eyebrows and appeared not to know the name.

'He was friends with Lord Arnulf,' I encouraged.

The mercers gave me the same response, appearing to search their memories and finding nothing similar that they could recall.

I thanked them for their efforts to help, but was not surprised when they moved away back to the bar: they saw little further trade coming their way from spending time with a lowly messenger.

Once they had gone, a tall, lean man sat down at my table. He was wearing a grey wool tunic and breeches. Damp dark grey curls and a full beard framed his long face, and a distinctive scar ran across his right cheek from his hazel eyes to his thin lips.

'I couldn't help but overhear you asking about the Lords Opecz and Arnulf,' he said softly, his hand covering his face so that others could not lipread what he said. 'The mercers did well from them, until they were forced to leave.'

'What made them go?'

'The Duke stripped them of their fiefs after he received too many complaints about them, their cruelty and mismanagement.'

The mercer in brown moved closer to our table as he waited for service at the bar. The man sitting opposite me changed the subject without changing manner or tone.

'I find the low country wool makes a better protection for the weather we've had today. And it lasts well: I've had this kirtle several years.'

'Would you be able to take me there tomorrow?'

He knew I meant the Duke's fiefs rather than the clothing shop and nodded.

'I'm staying here tonight, too. I'll take you there on my way home in the morning. If the rain stops.'

As he laughed at the weather's unpredictability, a servant placed my bowl of dumpling stew in front of me.

'I'll leave you to eat in peace,' said the tall, lean man. He disappeared back into the crowd.

I was up bright and early the next day after sleeping well. I paid extra for a breakfast to prepare for the day: more bread and cheese washed down with well water. When I went to the stable to saddle Finstar, the tall, lean man was already there saddling his own horse, a skewbald gelding.

'I thought you had changed your mind, Messenger,' he said, his voice still soft and low.

'What, and miss the opportunity to find myself a wool tunic as fine as yours?' I replied.

He laughed. 'At least the weather has improved. Let's go.'

I tipped the stable boy for the good care he had taken with Finstar overnight, and led my horse out behind the man and his horse into the courtyard of the inn. We mounted up and rode out into the cobbled street in single file. My guide led me through the town and into a busy marketplace. Half way along the bustling stalls, he pointed out a shop standing behind the traders.

'That's the place to go for good woollen clothes, all sorts of different cuts, designs and shades,' he said, 'But not today: it will be too busy.'

'Thank you. I will remember to call there the next time I am here,' I said.

He rode off into the crowd. I struggled to follow him with so many people crossing back and forth in front of Finstar's head. After a while, I feared I had mistaken his offer of help, and gave up. I rode Finstar out of the marketplace down a narrow alley into a square laid out around a public well. There on the far side of the square waited the tall, lean man on his skewbald horse.

He turned his horse half circle and rode off down the street on the far side of the square without giving me a glimmer of recognition. I followed, wondering what I was getting myself into. The horse and rider led the way through the streets to one of the city gates. He paused to nod to me to leave the city by the gate. Then he urged his horse down a narrow lane which ran along the inside of the city wall.

I did as he had indicated and turned left after going through the gates to follow a road outside the city walls which ran parallel to the one he had taken. Some distance later, I came to a three road junction where I had the choice of continuing along the walls or travelling away from the city across the fields towards the hills lying between Wohlstadt and distant Harzland.

At first, both roads seemed empty. But then I espied along the road heading into the country, the figure of a tall, lean man on a tall, lean horse, and followed.

He led me through fields and forests up into the foothills. Again, I feared he might be leading me into danger. He never looked back to see if I was still following, and he kept an even pace, as if he had many miles to go that day.

It was late morning when the road we took curled round the side of a hill and a vista spread below us of a secluded valley dotted with cottages and farmsteads. Ahead of us stood an old castle, with distinctive squat towers and shallow tiled roofs, linked by rubble-built walls that needed mortar to make them sturdy again. The road took us towards the castle, passing the ruins of two dwellings which looked as if they had burnt down some years before.

The tall, lean man rode past the castle gate, but halted and turned his horse to face me where the road went back into the forest. There he stood and waited while I rode up towards the castle entrance.

I would have ridden past the gateway as the pennants on the castle walls displayed the symbol of an argent bridge on sable. But then I noticed the capstones on the two stone gateposts. They bore the carved symbol of two crossed cleaver falchions. I turned to thank my guide, but he had vanished into the forest. Grateful for his assistance, I turned from the road and rode up to the gateway.

A wizened old gatekeeper walked out of a little cottage and stood in front of Finstar, blocking the entrance.

'What is your business, traveller?' he asked. His manner was more perfunctory than challenging.

I dismounted to speak to him, sensing he would be too astute to accept the tale I had told the mercers.

'I am Messenger Gendal. I was sent to enquire about Lord Arnulf's previous life.'

'Who wants to know?'

'The House of Harzberg where he now resides.'

'Ah,' said the gatekeeper with a knowing nod. 'Then you'd better bring your horse inside. I'll poker up the fire.'

He showed me where to stable Finstar and led me into his snug wattle and daub cottage, which lay tucked in among the trees behind the left gatepost. The cottage consisted of two rooms, one above the other. The downstairs room felt chilly with a draft coming in through the open window and door.

'Have to keep them open, to watch out for travelling folks like yourself,' the gatekeeper explained.

He drew up another stool to the fire and invited me to join him. As I moved the stool closer to the flames to warm myself, he made us mugs of hot sage and honey tea.

'Settle yourself down for a long tale, Messenger Gendal,' he began, slouching like a sack of logs over his stool. 'I have always been a gatekeeper here. In the days of my youth, the house of Arnulf Althaus was held in honour. Your Lord Arnulf is the third of that name. His father, Arnulf the Second, was renowned throughout the Duchy as a powerful but fair man. His grandfather, Arnulf the First, had fought bravely with the then Duke, who rewarded him with the fief and the family's coat of arms.'

'Were those curved blades in the falchion device what they actually fought with?'

'Yes, and butcher's cleavers too, I was told. They fought the Crusades, and they defended the Duke's lands, and luck and honour went with them wherever they went and whatever they did.'

'But then it went wrong?'

'Arnulf the Second bequeathed his son, the one you know, this fief, and great pride, and a love of combat. But he failed to teach him prudence, and loyalty, and respect for all God's creatures. When Arnulf the Third inherited this seat, he ruled it with a rod of iron. He showed no mercy to those he thought had wronged him. He had no understanding of the nature of farming, that for every good year there may be several poor years. And he mistreated his serfs cruelly. I only survived his reign because my job was simple: I followed his orders to admit those he wanted to see, and I closed the gates to those he told me to turn away.'

'So there were gates here once? What happened to them?'

'The Duke heard so many complaints against young Arnulf, he sent his bailiffs to investigate. I was ordered to keep the gates shut, which I did. So the Duke's men tore them down, and they've never been replaced. When Arnulf refused to submit to the Duke's men, he sent further forces to remove him. Then he gave the fief to our present lord, who is every bit as good as Arnulf is bad.'

'How long ago was this?'

'About six years ago, soon after the Feast of St Sylvester.'

'Did Arnulf have a friend called Lord Opecz?'

'He did, and the one was as bad as the other, so they say. If you are travelling back to Harzland from here, you are bound to go through Opecz's former fief too.'

'Was he also a tenant of the Duke of Romfeld?'

'He was, and the two were thick as thieves.'

I gave the gateman a halfpenny tip for answering all my questions so willingly. Before I left to travel on to Opecz's former fief, I asked the gateman one more question.

'Do you know who the man was on the skewbald horse, the one who led me here? And why did he act as if he didn't know me?'

'He still fears reprisals. Did you see the scar on his face? That was Arnulf's parting message to him.'

Chapter 10
The Boar Hunt

I left Rehschloss for Harzberg the day after I had returned from visiting the Duchy of Romfeld, six days after accepting Prince Oscar's invitation. My journey back to Sigmund's castle had taken me through Opecz's former fief, where I learned that he too had forfeited his lands because of his cruelty and mismanagement.

My findings did not surprise Dr Petrus. We retired to the library after dinner on the evening of my return, and sat in comfort by the fire, far away from the often brutal world outside.

'Wherever I went, I saw good lands ruined: homes and farmsteads destroyed by fire, villages with only men as they hid the womenfolk from strangers; scarred faces, missing hands, people trying to work their way back from destitution.'

'As I feared, Gendal.' Petrus sighed. 'Thank you for going to find out. That would explain the waves of refugees who flooded Harzland six years ago. And the Duke's expulsion of Arnulf and Opecz from their fiefs would explain their arrival in Harzberg later that year to join Prince Umbert's court.'

'There is one thing I don't understand, Doctor. If Opecz only came to Harzland six years ago, leaving behind such carnage in his old fief, how did he become Sheriff?'

'Well may you ask. From what I heard at that time, Opecz ingratiated himself with Prince Umbert. When the health of the previous Sheriff failed, a little unexpectedly, the Prince made Opecz sheriff instead. The former Sheriff died soon after, make of that what you will.'

His expression told me that the good doctor had no love for Opecz and considered him guilty of hastening the former Sheriff's death.

The next afternoon, Petrus and Dietl organised the servants to give me a lordly send of from Rehschloss. They all lined up on the steps of the Great Hall to wave me off. I took Goswin with me, as he would be expected to care for my needs while I stayed with Oscar, to lessen the workload of the castle's own servants at such a busy time.

It was a mild day, and I travelled light with arms, carrying my court robes and wearing my mail, gambeson and cloak to protect me from the dangers of the road. Goswin travelled even lighter, with no armour and just a horse, dagger and buckler borrowed from Rehschloss. Our journey passed without incident, and the city of Harzberg welcomed me with the same waves and cheers as they accorded the visiting nobility.

I arrived to find Harzberg Castle thronged by Oscar's relatives and in-laws. With little room to spare in the royal apartments, the Chamberlain placed me in one of the nursery rooms in the top storey. Though the bed and fittings were plain and scuffed by past generations of children, the room suited me well. It was a marked improvement on the inns that had provided my bed during my recent travels. The position of the room also made it nigh impossible for anyone to try the Rehschloss ghost trick on me again.

At the evening meal on the day of my arrival, the top table was so filled with Oscar's relatives that the Chamberlain and the Castellan had moved down off the dais to sit at a table headed by Opecz and Arnulf. My own seat was with the household cavalry again, closer to the dais than the men at arms. The horsemen and soldiers made merry company over the meal as they were looking forward to the sport the following day.

The morning of the boar hunt dawned dry with a light frost, which soon lifted as the sun rose higher in the sky. It was an ideal day for a winter hunt. The courtyard and the grassy ward thronged with people and creatures preparing to set out. A pack of hunting dogs deafened us with their yelping as their keepers readied them for the chase. The cavalrymen carried lugged boar spears and the men at arms bore hunting swords with blades broader near the tip than the haft. I carried both, all supplied from the castle armoury. Near where I waited on Finstar, archers and falconers mingled with the crowd of squires, pages, butchers and porters who would support us in the hunt.

Prince Oscar himself led us out of the castle on our quest. He was resplendent in a white velvet brigandine crested with the red Hart of Harzland, and rode a beautiful bay gelding controlled by decorated harnesses and covered in a short pale grey caparison decorated with his coat of arms.

Oscar led the hunt down the hillside into the beech forest, taking us all to a place where wild boar were often seen. On his signal, the dog handlers released their hounds to seek the scent of a boar. For a while, we heard only the rustling in the undergrowth as the dogs ran to and fro with muzzles down, trying to pick up the scent.

The dogs sprang forward into the forest, barking as they closed upon their quarry. We chased after them, the men on foot moving as quickly as those on horseback as we wove through the beech and oak trees. We heard the baying of the dogs change note as they trapped their quarry in a thicket. The cavalrymen spread out in a circle among the trees, ready to ambush a fleeing boar. The lead dog handler released the armoured catch dog into the thicket where the boar had turned at bay. Behind the catch dog ran the men at arms, brandishing their hunting swords.

The catch dog cornered the boar in the thicket and sank its teeth into his ear. The boar squealed and tossed his head about, trying to shake off the dog and throwing it against a tree trunk to force it to relax its jaws. The distraction enabled the men at arms to move much closer to the boar. One of the men leapt forward. With a practised swoop he thrust his sword into the beast's back. The sharp blade slid easily through the cape of fat over the boar's shoulders into his heart.

The beast fell to the ground, bleeding to death.

Our hunting party regrouped in a nearby clearing to celebrate the first kill. Oscar praised the huntsman who had executed the death-blow and rewarded him with a silver coin. Behind us, the butchers and porters went into the thicket to prepare the carcass and take it back to the castle kitchens. The hound-keepers checked their dogs for signs of injury. The first catch dog was retired for the day and the next catch dog chosen. Soon after the porters had taken the butchered carcass back to the castle, the hunt reformed to seek a second quarry.

Our tension mounted as the dogs scouted for scent. They led us deeper into the beech forest before their cry took up again. Our hunting party raced through the trees to corner our second boar that morning. This beast was more wily and rolled on the catch dog to force it to open its jaws to release his ear. The foot hunters sprang back, giving the boar too much space. He dodged through their cordon with just a nick on his flank and charged straight towards the knights. They rode against his path with great horse control, jabbing their boar spears into his side as he dashed past them. He fell, panting with pain, bleeding from copious wounds, with three boar spears firmly embedded in his sides. The foot hunters closed in warily to finish off the dying beast.

Over the course of the day, I watched the prowess of the young hunters with increasing respect as they proved their bravery and skill again and again. This was a truly great way for them to practice their battle tactics in situations of real danger. Between them they killed four boars by mid-afternoon, while Prince Oscar observed them from the rear of the field accompanied by Heinrich and those relatives who enjoyed the excitement of engaging in a hunt while not putting themselves at any risk.

After the fourth kill, Oscar ordered the trumpeter to sound the signal to return to the castle, and turned his horse in that direction. As we turned to follow, a boar ran out from cover ahead of us, running down the hill straight for our party. Only two of us were carrying both boar spears and swords: Klaus and myself.

'Aside!' I ordered the field; 'Klaus, in with me!'

Prince Oscar turned his horse too sharply out of the path of the boar. The bay gelding shied, throwing him from his saddle. Klaus and I rode our horses towards the boar from either side to draw it away from Oscar. The beast turned on us but dithered between which of us to charge first. Klaus threw his spear at the boar and turned his horse aside to avoid colliding with me. The boar spun round towards him as the spear pierced its shoulder cape. The blade fell off, pulled out by its weight.

I rode past on the boar's other side and pushed my spear through its shoulders into its ribs. After the pass, I coaxed Finstar back round to meet the boar's path. I awaited my moment to leap from the saddle with the hunting sword in my hand. Using double handed force, I rammed the blade through the boar's shoulder cape to finish it off. The beast's momentum took it a few steps further down the hill before it keeled over onto its knees and collapsed, bleeding to death.

Klaus rode over to my side and clapped me on the shoulder.

'Never again shall I tease you for your lance skills, Gendal!'

'Your distraction helped me land the crucial blow, Klaus.'

I caught hold of Finstar's reins, rubbed his nose and hugged his neck to thank him for responding so well to the challenge. Then Klaus and I rode back to the royal party, which had regrouped on a track further up the hill. Oscar was sitting rigidly on his beautiful bay gelding, still startled by the closeness of the averted danger.

'By your leave, Prince Oscar, shall Knight Klaus and I escort you back to Harzberg Castle?' I asked.

He nodded wordlessly, his face showing his relief as he accepted our solution. He rode between us in silence back up the hill. The rest of his party followed, discussing at length the surprising spectacle of the fifth kill.

Chapter 11
The Hunt Ball

That night, Klaus and I were the darlings of the hunt ball. We were both given seats of honour near the centre of the top table. Oscar placed Klaus on his left with Herlinde, while I sat on Oscar's right with sour-faced Heinrich on my other side. Our inclusion forced the prince's other relatives to sit closer together. To ease the crush, some chose to sit on the tables below the dais with the household cavalry and senior officers instead.

We feasted on the fresh boar meat the hunt had provided that day: a cheerful addition to the advent fare of pease pottage and rye bread. Oscar dined royally on the flesh of the boar which had charged him, washed down with copious amounts of his land's wine.

'I now see why the Imperator thought to ennoble you, Gendal. Your quick wits and bravery are a credit to our court.'

'Thank you, Prince Oscar. But though knight I am, I am no noble, just Ministerialis with the quick wits gained on the road. You have many fine young knights here who showed equal bravery today.'

'But not with equal results.'

He drank another draft from his goblet. I used the opportunity to take out the letter Prince Volkmar had asked me to deliver to him in person.

'Your Highness, before I left Schwarzenberg, Prince Volkmar gave me this letter to bring to you.'

He frowned. 'Why did you not give me this before?'

'The conditions Prince Volkmar gave me had not occurred before now, your Highness.'

He laughed. 'Typical of him! He loves to meddle.'

He broke the seal on the letter and read the contents, holding the paper away from me to stop me reading it too. A look of concern passed across his face as he folded the letter and put it away in the pouch attached to his belt.

'You have clearly impressed my great uncle too, Gendal. He asks me to give you every assistance.' His face brightened. 'How do you find Rehschloss? Is it to your liking?'

'I like it very much, your highness. Your old tutor, Dr Petrus, makes an agreeable companion, and Steward Dietl manages the castle and the estate very well.'

'We are glad you have chosen to take up the bequest and settle there.' He chewed a chunk of roasted boar, swallowed, and washed it down with more wine. 'Dr Petrus... I hadn't realised he is still alive. Perhaps he would tutor our children, too.'

'I am sure he would be honoured to give you that service.'

'Do you have children, Gendal?'

'I am not even married, nor do I seek a wife.'

'Ah, you are missing out on one of life's greatest joys.'

'Perhaps the one who is not my spouse is missing some of life's greatest sorrows,' I replied with a smile.

Oscar laughed and slapped his thigh in an over-appreciative response to my jest.

The way the Prince was drinking, I feared he would soon be too drunk to observe the traditions of a court ball. Heavy drinking seemed to be common in his family. Concerned he would not last the night, I asked a question to prompt him to move on the proceedings.

'Prince Oscar, this is the first time I have attended a solstice celebration here. What does it entail?'

'Now that we have eaten, we will hold the dance. They should clear the tables for that soon. Later tonight, we will light the bonfire to help the sun rise from the world of the dead tomorrow.'

He beckoned a server over and gave him instructions. Soon, the team of servers cleared the tables and moved them closer to the walls. Other servants swept away the straw strewn across the flagstones to clear the dance floor. Musicians appeared in the gallery high in the wall at the far end of the hall, carrying bagpipes, recorder, drums, shawm, fiddle and harp. Prince Oscar rose to start off the dance, and everyone present rose too. As his wife was absent again, he offered his hand to his mother, Herlinde. She graciously permitted him to escort her onto the empty dance floor.

The musicians played a courtly version of a local folk song, slowing down the tempo to transform it into a measured promenade. Oscar moved through the motions of the dance, elegantly guided by Herlinde, who had to support him through some of the turns. As she steered him back towards the dais after just one circuit of the floor, the music increased in speed and other couples came out to take up the dance started by their Lord and Prince.

Oscar slumped back in his carver chair and reached for his goblet of wine.

'Shall we try our luck with the ladies?' Klaus asked me: 'We shall never have a better time than this.'

I followed him off the dais onto the dance floor only because the members of the court would expect of me to join in. All I could think about was the prank Klaus had played on me at Rehschloss. I could not resist making a sly comment.

'How cold did your hands get, carrying the ice, Klaus?'

He looked at me in surprise and bewilderment. Then his face cleared. 'Oh, you mean the frosty reception after I helped you leave after your last visit? It was nothing. Lady Herlinde put everything right. You did impress me today, how you handled that boar spear.'

'Your quick wits impressed me – how you guessed my intentions and carried through with it.'

'You taught me a lot on our trip to Schwarzenberg.'

Klaus stopped at the head of one of the floor tables where several young maidens sat, chaperoned by their parents. The young women wore no head-coverings and had decorated their long hair with slender strands of braid. Klaus gave them one of his winning smiles, and two young ladies stood up at once to join us in the dance.

The lady who paired with me was slender and fair of face, with long brown hair and a mischievous smile. She wore a gown of green velvet edged with a trim of embroidered blue flowers, her own exquisite work.

'Everyone is talking about how brave you were, Knight Gendal. I shall be quite the object of envy, being the first lady to partner you in the dance,' she said. She had a coquettish way of looking sideways up at me with her head lowered so that I could see her long eyelashes and the pale complexion of her skin.

'What is your name?' I asked, keeping my manner polite and distant.

'Aglé Moltké,' she said with a giggle.

Her manner was all I detested in court circles, though it would surely find favour with others. I was relieved when the dance ended and I could return her to her table. I escaped to the dais and asked Herlinde if she would like me to partner her in a dance.

She looked across to her son for approval because of our great gulf in rank. He was half-slumped in his carver chair, oblivious to everything around him. She then looked for her brother Heinrich, but he was elsewhere. Having observed her obligations, she accepted my invitation with a smile.

'I see you are always on duty, Gendal,' she said as we paused at the edge of the dance floor for the other couples to make a space for us to join in. Her deep, melodic voice was so soothing, I could have listened to her for hours.

'I still keep your nosegay, Lady Herlinde,' I said, to avoid answering her. 'Mint and sage: virtue and wisdom. Did you choose them for a reason, or just because they are all that is still in season?'

'Even the mint has gone,' she replied.

We stepped into the dance and performed the pattern in formation with the other couples on the floor. Herlinde moved with grace and elegance. I felt as clumsy as a bear beside her. Though she clearly enjoyed dancing, it soon tired her. At her request, we returned to the dais to sit and watch the next dance, with Oscar sprawled between us, slouching over his goblet of wine.

'Gendal, you have now brought two sons back to me,' she said lightly.

Her face fell as Oscar slumped across the table, his face nearly landing on his plate.

'Don't worry, my Lady. He will be fine tomorrow. That is how shock takes some men.'

'Had he been in any real danger?'

'There is always real danger in a boar hunt. It is where young knights prove themselves when there is no war to fight.'

I caught the eye of a server and gestured to him to help Prince Oscar leave the ball. Across the hall, Heinrich saw my signal and hurried over, intending to object. When he saw the nature of the problem, his manner changed. He woke Oscar and persuaded the drunk prince to leave the hall with him. After they had gone, Herlinde sat in Oscar's place, by my side.

'Oh, to have had a child like you, Gendal. Your mother was very blessed.'

I nodded, and refrained from telling her my mother had paid a travelling messenger to take me away as a child because she and her village thought I was cursed.

'Have you forgiven me now?' I asked.

'Oscar thought you disliked him. He said it showed in your eyes. He thought you had believed Sigmund's stories about him and had taken Sigmund's side.'

'Was that the cause of the frosty reception the last time I was here?'

Herlinde nodded. 'You shamed him again when you saved him today: your bravery made his fear look like cowardice.'

'It must have been hard for him growing up in Sigmund's shadow, always second best. But Sigmund could never have been the ruler your son Oscar has become. Oscar is happy to live here with his people, whereas Sigmund never liked administration and detail – he would always have been away adventuring.'

'Do you really think so?'

'Aye, I do. Earlier this year, I fought alongside people who were destitute through the unreasonable greed of their ruler, Duke Nicolaus of Danuvia. When I came here, I saw the happy people in the streets; even the peasants are well dressed and well fed. That was the real contrast. Prince Oscar may not have expected to wear the crown, but he rules with respect and compassion for his people. This ball is a pale shadow of the balls held by Duke Nicolaus, but it is still just as entertaining, and at least no-one has been beggared to provide for it.'

The call came up to go out into the courtyard. The Great Hall emptied of people. I offered to escort Herlinde outside after the crowd. As I made the offer, Heinrich rudely pushed me aside, having come back after helping Oscar. I stepped away without taking offence and left the Great Hall alone to join the throng in the courtyard.

A towering bonfire stood unlit in the centre of the yard. The guests gathered round the pile to make a full circle. The Castellan crouched down at the base and struck a flint to make a spark among some dry leaves, creating a fragile yellow flame. As the leaves caught alight and curled, he placed more kindling around them to coax the bonfire into life. The twigs and sticks quickly blazed. He lit torches from their flames and handed them to his helpers to set fire to other parts of the tower of wood. Within a few minutes, the solstice bonfire blazed with heat and light, the symbolic new fire born from a tiny spark to mark the dawning of the new pagan year.

The crowd of people joined hands to sing and dance around the blaze. Their traditional carol was accompanied by the roar and crackle of the fire and the pungent wood smoke which billowed into the heavens. The words of their song were based on a folk spell to waken the weak sun in the morning, and to make it grow over the months ahead from its winter infancy into the maturity of summer.

As we danced and sang in our pre-Christian rite, the Matins bell rang in the nearby monastery, calling the monks to sing their offices and pray for the fallen world outside their walls, at the start of another solar year.

Chapter 12
The Witness of The Lesser Hall

I looked out of my chamber window late the next morning to see the remnants of the bonfire staining the cobbled courtyard below me. Already, servants worked around the blackened footprint of the fire, clearing up the ash and charcoal left there.

Two full days lay ahead before Christmas Eve, with its own rituals and traditions. The expectations were for guests to spend these days socialising with Oscar's family. Instead I chose to use them to find out more about Umbert's death and the part Sigmund played.

After exercising Finstar with the household cavalry, I spent time alone in the Lesser Hall, surrounded by the rich tapestries of heroes from history and legend. Goswin insisted on lighting a fire for me in the broad stone fireplace, fetching wood and kindling which he stacked by the hearth with the skills he had learned as a kitchen boy. To light the fire, he fetched a taper which had been lit from an oil lamp in the kitchen. This lamp burned the eternal flame which would not be extinguished until the next winter solstice at the end of the coming year, 1320. After Goswin had attended to my creature comforts, I sent him to find out who else had been staying in the castle at the beginning of May.

I sat at the head of the table where Oscar and Umbert had once sat and prayed for insight to unravel the truth of Umbert's death. The cold wood beneath me seemed to press upwards against my body rather than support the weight that bore down on it. If only the furniture could have told me what had really happened that May day.

I knew Sigmund would not have murdered his father to gain the crown, because he had never wanted that sort of power and authority. The status he had sought was to become a renowned hero, but as the crusades to the Holy Land had ended before he had come of age, he had been a hero without a cause until I took him to his death at Dernfels. But if Sigmund had not committed the deed deliberately, who or what had killed Umbert?

The hall felt abandoned after Goswin had gone to carry out my instructions. No-one disturbed my vigil at the battered and stained old table. No rushes or straw lay strewn across the floor, suggesting that the Lesser Hall had fallen out of use since Umbert had died there.

I tried to visualise the scene: Umbert sitting where I sat with Sigmund to my left. Petrus had said that people had accused Sigmund of poisoning his father. How? With food? With drink? With a poisoned dagger? Did someone else witness the act, or were they alone together when the deed occurred?

Needing more information about that crucial meeting between father and son, I pulled open the entrance doors by their heavy brass knobs and looked out across the courtyard. I had hoped to see Goswin or one of the servants whom I could send to fetch one of the family members who had stayed there in May. To my dismay I saw Aglé and her sister. They had just left the Great Hall on some errand, and both of them had noticed me.

'Knight Gendal,' Aglé greeted with great enthusiasm.

She trotted across to speak to me with her sister firmly in tow. She was still wearing the green gown she had worn the night before, but her hair was more plainly dressed.

'Lady Aglé,' I replied formally.

'But what are you doing here, in this empty old place? Has no-one told you they don't use this hall any more?'

She looked me in the face and blushed. Indeed, she blushed every time she looked me in the face, as if she had been smitten with a girlish infatuation for me.

'I was trying to understand what happened, Lady Aglé. Would you like to introduce me to your sister?'

'How did you know we were sisters?' She giggled. 'This is my biggest sister, Marlena.'

'Lady Marlena,' I said with a courteous bow.

Marlena looked a more rounded and mature version of Aglé, with gleaming chestnut hair and an even oval face.

'My sister sings your praises, Knight Gendal, and not just for saving our Prince Oscar.'

'That, I'm sure, is undeserved. May I ask a favour of you both? If you see my page Goswin while on your errands, could you please send him here to me? I would like to speak to someone who was present when Prince Umbert died.'

'If you are wondering what happened, perhaps we can help,' Marlena offered.

I stood back from the door to let the sisters in, but made sure the door stayed open while they were with me. The little warmth in the hall soon dissipated with the additional draft which came in through the open door and left straight out up the chimney, taking with it the heat and flames.

We gatherer round the head of the table where Umbert had died. As I questioned the two sisters about the events on May Day, elder Marlena talked while younger Aglé giggled, flirted, and batted her eyelids at me.

'Were you both present the day Prince Umbert died?'

'We both took part in the maying party. But no-one was present here when Prince Sigmund did the deed. We were all in the courtyard, dismounting after the ride.'

'When did you first realise something was wrong?'

'The door was open, as it is now. We heard raised voices, mainly Prince Umbert's. There was a lot of noise outside. We couldn't hear what he was saying. But we all heard the strangled cry, and Sigmund shouting out, "Father!"'

Marlena's face clouded as she recalled the scene. She continued, 'Two courtiers ran in – I think they were Sheriff Opecz and Lord Arnulf. They saw Sigmund sitting with his arm around his father's shoulder, holding a goblet of wine to his lips. Then Umbert made a strange gurgling noise. One of them dashed the goblet to the ground. He shouted out, "You've poisoned him!" But it was too late. Prince Umbert had already drunk the potion. Though they sent for Brother Matthias to help him, within hours he was dead.'

Marlena turned to look at the table and chair with an air of sorrow and disappointment.

'We had all rushed in. The Lords were accusing Sigmund of murder. Sigmund and Oscar both looked shocked. Lady Herlinde screamed. She ran to cradle Umbert in her arms and tried to will him back to life. Heinrich took charge and sent us all to our rooms. Sheriff Opecz picked up the goblet and smelled the dregs in it. He threw it down and then he questioned Oscar and Sigmund.'

'Do you remember where the goblet landed?'

Marlena shook her head. Aglé just giggled. I asked them to sit at the table. Aglé took Umbert's place at the head of the table, and Marlena sat where Sigmund had, to Umbert's left.

'So Sigmund had his right arm around his father's shoulders, and he held the goblet in his left hand,' I said. 'Were there any other things on the table? A flagon perhaps, or a second goblet?'

Marlena reflected and shook her head. 'I can't remember.'

'There was another goblet,' Aglé said, and giggled. 'Prince Umbert and Prince Sigmund had both been drinking again. That's why they had got so cross.'

'That is helpful, Lady Aglé. Do you remember where Sigmund's goblet landed when the courtier dashed it to the ground?'

'Behind him?' Aglé suggested, too eager to please to be accurate.

I thanked them both for letting me intrude upon their morning and walked to the open door to encourage them to leave.

As Aglé passed me on the way out of the door, she whispered, 'I'll see you tonight,' and giggled. Marlena scolded her with a fierce look and propelled her into the courtyard.

After they had gone, I shut the door and sat back where Umbert had sat when he had quaffed his last drink. Goswin came in a short while later, bringing me a tray of food for lunch: bread and slices of cold boar meat, an apple and a mug of mint tea.

'Ah, Goswin, I am right glad to see you. What have you found out for me?'

My young page recited a list of all the people who had stayed at Harzberg Castle on May Day while I ate. Many were family members who were already staying in the castle again for the Christmas season. The rest were due to arrive in the next two days. Most were relatives: the rest were from well-bred families with marriageable daughters, like the Moltkés with Marlena and Aglé.

Recalling Aglé's parting promise with a shudder, I said, 'Goswin, I want you to sleep in my chamber tonight, for my protection. Make up a couch for yourself by the door. Be quiet about it. I don't want other people to know.'

'Of course, Sir,' he said, looking very surprised: 'But how can I protect you? - any more than you can defend yourself? I've not been trained to fight.'

'Not every battle is fought with strength,' I said, hoping my measures would prove unnecessary.

Goswin stoked the fire and left the chilly hall to carry out my instructions. I sat at the table and continued to reflect in thoughtful silence.

A short while later, the door opened to admit Sheriff Opecz and Lord Arnulf. Their confident presence filled the draughty hall, making it feel much smaller. They were tall, well-muscled, and well dressed for the cold weather, wearing padded jerkins and leggings, riding boots and long cloaks. Neither wore the Hart surcoats of Harzland over their jerkins: though they attended the court at Harzberg, they were independent lords in their own right.

'Knight Gendal, Lady Marlena asked us to come here to speak with you,' said Opecz. His face was shrewd and his manner was that of someone used to commanding men and being obeyed. 'I was the one who arrested Prince Sigmund after the murder.'

'Thank you for indulging me with your presence, Lord Opecz,' I said.

'The ladies told us you wanted to know where the goblet landed when I struck it out of the murderer Sigmund's hand,' Arnulf said.

Their judgemental statements made me wonder whether they were fully convinced of Sigmund's guilt, or rather just wanted to convince me of it. Arnulf's lean face had a calculating expression which made his even features less than becoming.

'Why are you raking up all this old scandal?' demanded Opecz; 'Sigmund is dead. Oscar is crowned. Nothing you hear will change that.'

I played with the Imperator's ring on the middle finger of my left hand. The wordless gesture made its mark. Opecz felt the need to justify himself before me in deference to my imputed influence.

'Sigmund absconded before we could take him to be judged by his peers and the King of Rome.'

'And if you had taken him, what evidence would you have brought to substantiate your claim?' I asked.

'We had the cup, we had the man, and we had a crowd of witnesses to their argument beforehand,' said Arnulf.

'I see. Where did the cup land?'

Arnulf pointed to the floor, about a foot away from the middle of the table on the side that Sigmund had sat.

'That would have taken some force for the cup to land there. Did you strike it aside with your hand, or wrest it from Sigmund's grip?'

'I struck it,' Arnulf said. He demonstrated his backhanded blow menacingly close to my face.

'So you risked striking Prince Umbert to knock the cup away,' I stated, unmoved.

'It was necessary, to try to save him.'

'Was there wine in the cup?'

'I can't remember! Why all these questions?'

'These are the questions you would have faced had you brought Sigmund before the King of Rome. His lawyers are very astute.'

'There was some wine in the cup,' Opecz said to take the pressure off Arnulf. 'It spilt across the table. The cup bounced on the floor before it came to rest.'

'And where is the cup now?'

Both looked at each other in surprise.

'Back in the kitchens, I would presume,' said Opecz; 'There was no need to keep it after Sigmund absconded.'

'I see. Where do you think Sigmund obtained the poison you say he put in the cup?'

'How should we know? Some wise woman?' Arnulf said.

'So Sigmund had the forethought to procure some poison before he argued with Umbert?' I replied.

'Yes, he got the poison and then caused the argument,' Arnulf said. 'He tried to claim his father died of natural causes, but it was obvious: he wanted the throne.'

I nodded. 'And did you find the phial containing the poison?'

Opecz reluctantly admitted, 'No, we did not.'

'Thank you, my Lords. I shall take up no more of your time,' I said to dismiss them.

They left, with a glittering anger in their eyes that warned me my questions had just made me two enemies.

Chapter 13
An Unexpected Summons

As I left the Lesser Hall that afternoon, a lady-in-waiting came across the courtyard to speak to me. She was younger than Lady Herlinde's ladies-in-waiting, and I had not seen her before. Her gown was well-tailored in red and maroon brocade, and a white silk wimple covered her hair and framed her face.

'There you are, Knight Gendal. If it please you, pray come with me,' she said with a curtsey.

Intrigued, I followed her into the Great Hall and up the staircase. Instead of turning left on the first floor to enter the Royal Apartments, she turned right and push open a stiff wooden door. We emerged in a long solarium bright with winter sunlight shining through the large leaded glass windows. The small clear diamond-shaped panes magnified the rays of the weak sun and helped to make the room warmer than the heat provided by the two fireplaces. The bright, airy chamber was large enough for the ladies of the house to promenade when the weather outside was inclement.

A young woman stood up to greet me. Her build was slight but for the swelling of her pregnant belly. She was dainty and fair, with an almost ethereal beauty. Her maternity gown was of embroidered cream silk, and she wore an intricate lace head-covering to satisfy the convention for a married woman to conceal her hair.

'Princess Eleanore,' I greeted, bowing low.

As I straightened, her pale blue eyes regarded me with that same look I had seen twice before: once on the day I had arrived, looking down on me from a high window as I crossed the courtyard; and the second time from another window as I walked with Lady Herlinde in the herb garden. Here was the mysterious person who had watched me and followed my early progress at Harzberg.

Eleanore sat back down in her wooden armchair, which she had made comfortable with red silk cushions. The lady-in-waiting sat behind me in another chair. They had both been making lace, and the tables and frames holding the delicate fabrics they fashioned lay forgotten beside them.

'Knight Gendal, thank you for coming at my summons. I understand you have been asking questions about the death of my father-in-law, Prince Umbert. I believe I can assist you.'

I wondered how she had come by that information. My surprise must have shown on my face, for she explained:

'The window glass is thin. We spend most of our days in here, and we hear almost everything people say in the courtyard below.'

'You are very astute, Princess Eleanore. I thank you for doing me the honour of arranging this interview. I had begun to wonder if you even existed.'

She laughed, a beautiful silvery laugh. 'My husband Oscar is very protective of me. He likes to keep me out of harm's way. He does not know I wished to see you, and I would like it to stay that way.'

'I am at your service, Ma'am. I promise to keep our meeting between us three alone.'

She read my face correctly again and answered my unspoken question.

'Think not that I fear Oscar. My husband is a good man, and I have no complaint about him. I want him to have no complaint about me.'

'Your loyalty is commendable, Ma'am.'

'I believe you are looking for a vessel, Knight Gendal – the cup my father-in-law Prince Umbert drank from when he died.'

She brought out a goblet from a shelf beneath her lace-making table and placed it on the table.

'How did you know I was looking for that, Ma'am?' I asked in surprise.

I reached for the goblet. She nodded her approval for me to pick it up and inspect it. The cup was made of silver, decorated with garnets and lapis lazuli. The rim was slightly misshapen, as if someone had thrown it against a hard surface with great force. Dried traces of red wine stained the inside of the cup.

'Your meeting with Lord Opecz and Lord Arnulf greatly angered them, Gendal. I would have thought the whole castle heard their protests about the closeness of your questioning over the goblet and its contents, not just us here in this high room.'

'Perhaps I was a little hard on them. How came you by this?'

'I was one of the first people to enter the hall after Opecz and

Arnulf. I saw the goblet lying on the rushes. They shouted "murderer!" and arrested Sigmund. As he was the man I had expectations of marrying, I wanted to protect him. So I picked up the goblet and hid it in my skirts.'

'I don't understand, Ma'am. You had expectations of marrying Sigmund, but now you are married to Oscar?'

'Very happily married, and I shall shortly bear his child. Do you understand marriage alliances, Gendal?'

'Indeed, I do, Ma'am. I served our last Imperator as Ministerialis. I heard his lawyers explain some of the niceties of marriage contracts on several occasions.'

The reply made her smile as she imagined the verbose explanations of the lawyers. She spoke on.

'Prince Umbert arranged an alliance between my family, the Boesels, and his family, the Hirschmanns, that I should marry the Crown Prince. At the time of the agreement, Sigmund was Crown Prince, and I was very happy at the prospect of marrying him.'

She looked away to give herself time to frame her next statement.

'Unfortunately, Sigmund was not happy at the prospect of marrying me, or indeed any woman. So I was the cause of the argument between father and son, which left the elder dead and the one I loved discredited.'

'That must be a heavy burden to bear. What do you think happened that day?'

She sighed and turned away to hider her frustration at her lack of insight.

'If only I could answer that!' she cried, and turned back to face me. 'I have thought about it time after time, but cannot go beyond my own guilt. I do not know why Prince Umbert died. But I cannot believe Sigmund killed his father. I knew him well. He was an honourable man. He just didn't want to get married.'

A tear rolled down her left cheek. She paused from speaking to compose herself. I looked down at my feet to let her save face.

'Do not think that I despise my husband,' she said at length. 'Oscar became the Crown Prince, who I was contracted to marry. We wed in June. I have found him to be a good man too now that he is out of his brother's shadow, and I am content to be his wife.'

I looked out of the large window, much as Eleanore had done, and felt a deep sorrow for her in her situation, but also a great respect for the way she comported herself in such circumstances.

'Keep the goblet, Knight Gendal. Go and prove Sigmund's innocence. For my sake, and for Lady Herlinde, clear his name even though he is dead.'

She sobbed deeply. Her lady-in-waiting put an arm around her shoulders to comfort her. She gave me a silent nod to tell me to go.

Chapter 14
An Unexpected Accusation

Next morning, I rode out with the household cavalry to exercise Finstar with their horses. We arrived back to hear the Sext service bell ringing in the nearby Cistercian monastery, which stood about a mile away along the valley behind Harzberg. The monastery's service bells helped to regulate the life in the castle and the town as well as the cloisters. I decided to attend Vespers that evening as it was Sunday, knowing that the business of Christmas Eve would take up most of my time and patience the following day. I also hoped the

Abbot would let me speak to Brother Matthias, the monk who had b treated Umbert on the day of his death.

My night's sleep had been disturbed, as I had feared, by a nocturnal visitor. During the darkest hour of the night, someone tried to open our bedroom door. As the door had no lock, I had secured it by placing Goswin's couch across the doorway to block any movement. The door thudded against his bed several times before the intruder realised the way was barred.

'Sir Gendal,' whispered a woman, her giggle and her tone of voice intending to allure.

Goswin swore. The door tapped against his couch again.

'Stop pushing! That's my bed you're hitting,' he shouted.

A gasp of surprise came from the other side of the door.

'Return to your chamber, Lady Aglé,' I ordered; 'There is nothing that cannot wait until morning.'

The door shut with a thud and the faintest of footsteps walked away.

'Thank you, Goswin,' I said with a wry laugh; 'You have saved two people's reputations this night, just by being here.'

'So that's what you meant, Sir, when you said I could protect you.'

I rolled over to go back to sleep and slept well enough after the incident. The bags under Goswin's eyes next morning showed he had not. He was still yawning when I handed Finstar's reins to him after returning from riding out with the cavalry.

'After you have sorted Finstar, Goswin, go and have a nap,' I ordered.

He nodded gratefully, but before he could lead Finstar away, another page marched up to us and pointed his finger at me.

'This is the one!' he accused.

'The one who what?' I asked.

'The one who tried to injure Prince Oscar in the night!'

I looked at Goswin in surprise as Heinrich and Sheriff Opecz joined us.

'Arrest this man!' Heinrich ordered.

'On what charge?' I asked.

'Attacking Prince Oscar in the night,' Heinrich stated.

'And who makes this accusation?'

'How do you plead?' demanded Opecz.

A circle of knights and horsemen gathered round us, curious to see the outcome of this unexpected challenge.

'Before I make any attempt to answer the charge, I insist on knowing who makes the accusation, Lord Heinrich,' I said.

Arnulf pushed through the crowd. He had also ridden out with us and was wearing a plain grey surcoat over his mail. It was similar to the surcoat worn by the knight who had attacked me in the training field soon after I first arrived in Harzland. The hairs on my back and neck prickled in the face of this potential new danger.

'I make the accusation,' Arnulf said. 'I awoke in the night and saw Knight Gendal creeping away from Prince Oscar's chamber after the traitorous deed.'

'But that's not true!' Goswin protested.

'Do you want to be arrested with your master?' Heinrich warned.

I looked up at the solarium and saw Eleanore's eyes looking down at us all in the courtyard. The scene had already attracted others, including most of the household cavalry and the Chamberlain.

'My Lords, let us take this argument out of the courtyard and into the Great Hall, where we may be a little more private and certainly a lot warmer. Goswin, come with us,' I stated firmly, in a louder voice than I normally used. It was the firm tone of command I employed rarely on those few occasions I wanted others to obey.

My manner had the desired effect. The leading participants walked off into the Great Hall. Klaus and the young cavalrymen trailed in behind them. Heinrich tried to stop them.

'Sheriff Opecz, order the cavalry out of the hall, before they turn this into a complete spectacle,' he ordered.

'No, let them stay too,' I said, knowing I had far less to hide than my accusers.

'At what time of the night did this happen?' asked the Chamberlain.

'Do not answer, Lord Arnulf. It is my place as Sheriff to ask the questions, not others,' said Opecz.

'It is my right to be told about all that happens in the Royal Apartments,' insisted the Chamberlain.

The two men glared at each other. Each was clearly trying to protect his own area of authority. It reassured me to discover that not everyone approved of Opecz.

'Well, what time of the night did it happen?' asked Klaus, breaking through their impasse.

His involvement surprised me, having classed him as Heinrich's lackey. It also surprised Heinrich, who glared at him, and Opecz, who did not censure his intervention.

'While it was dark,' Arnulf stated with a scowl.

'Then how did you see it was Knight Gendal?' Klaus asked.

'I saw the face in the candlelight.'

I struggled not to laugh. Arnulf had had no cause to discover yet that one of my skills is the ability to move silently through buildings and byways in the dark.

'Goswin, tell everyone where you were last night,' I ordered.

The lad moved to the front of the crowd. He trembled visibly as he answered.

'I slept in Knight Gendal's room, as I was told to. My bed blocked the door. My master could not have left without waking me and moving my bed.'

'How convenient!' scowled Heinrich. 'Do you really expect us to believe that?'

'Go and look: the couch is still there,' I replied. 'One of the ladies staying here expressed her amorous intentions towards me. As there are no door locks, I made such provision as I could to protect us both from scandal.'

The cavalrymen laughed heartily at this. Heinrich glared at Arnulf in embarrassment for being caught out pursuing a false charge. Opecz looked disappointed by the success of my alibi. Arnulf's face blackened deeper, as if he intended further spite after being foiled in his plot.

'If that is all, sirs, Goswin and I will go and tend my horse,' I said.

I took Goswin's shoulders and guided him out through the crowd. The cavalrymen moved aside to clear our way, and some clapped my shoulder in support. No-one tried to stop us.

Out in the courtyard, I sensed we were being observed and glanced back. Once again, Princess Eleanore was watching events from her vantage point at the solarium window. Perhaps it was my imagination, but I thought her expression showed relief.

I spent much of the rest of the day talking to everyone in the castle who had stayed there for the maying holiday, and who was willing to talk to me. From guests to servants, the witnesses gave me little information that was new, but what they did say tended to corroborate Princess Eleanore's version of events rather than Arnulf's and Opecz's.

Late that afternoon, I set off on foot for the Cistercian monastery where Brother Matthias lived and worked. He was the one person I had not yet met who might possibly hold the key to the puzzle I was trying to solve. The broad road led me there through the forest of bare oak and beech trees. It felt good to spend some time alone with my thoughts as I strolled between the impassive trees.

The monastery had a high stone curtain wall with stout corner towers protecting the cloisters, gardens and the abbey church inside. The main entrance was an arched gate with two heavy wooden doors which stayed shut even during the day. Further round the wall, a small wooden door gave local people access to the abbey church during the monks' singing of the offices. As I was too early for the evening office of Vespers, that door was also shut.

I returned to the main gate and pulled on the handle which hung on the left side of the gateway. A bell rang somewhere close by inside the walls. After a brief wait, a monk opened a small barred hatch in the door to speak to me.

'Can I speak to Brother Matthias?' I asked.

'Does someone need his services?'

'No. I seek the truth behind Prince Umbert's death. I believe he can help me.'

'Go round to the church door. Someone will let you in. We will ask Brother Matthias if he wishes to speak to you.'

The hatch banged shut. I walked back round to the abbey entrance. After another brief wait, the monk on door-keeping duty admitted me. I deposited my weapons with him and crossed the green to the nave door to enter the shadowed stillness of the church.

Inside, the stone building felt cold but also safe. The stout

Romanesque arches were lit by a few torches whose flames made shadows play across the stonework, creating dark chasms in the heights. I felt a great heaviness, as though the high vaulted roof above was crowding down on me behind the darkness. A faint scent of incense pervaded the air, hinting at other more exotic realms and coaxing me to leave my worldly concerns behind.

A monk approached from the gloom of the choir, his white habit giving the impression of a ghostly figure until he drew closer.

'I am Brother Matthias. Do you have need of my skills?'

His voice was gentle, with the soothing tonal depth of a man of great faith.

'Thank you for seeing me, Brother Matthias. I seek not your skills but your memories, about the death of Prince Umbert.'

He sat down on my pew and drew back his hood so that I could see his clean-shaven face. It was the face of a person who had lived long and seen much suffering, with deeply etched lines in the leathery skin, yet made beautiful by the light of compassion in his eyes.

'Knight Gendal. I had hoped to meet you.'

'You know my name?'

'We withdraw from the world here, but we still serve the world. News does reach us behind these walls and guides our prayers. What would you like to know?'

'What do you think caused Prince Umbert's death?'

He smiled at my directness, and answered with the same.

'Apoplexy. Umbert sinned in his anger and God struck him down.'

'What made you come to that conclusion?'

'The sudden way he became paralysed: first one side of his body, and then the other; and how he choked on the drink he took.'

'Could any medicine or potion you know of have had the same effect?'

'No. Henbane and hemlock can cause death by paralysis, but both would cause other symptoms as well. None of the people present reported those too.'

'What did you feel when the Sheriff ignored your opinion and arrested Prince Sigmund for murdering his father?'

'I am only required to speak the truth as I see it. It is up to God to influence the minds of those who hear it, not me.'

He looked more closely at me and seemed to absorb some of the great weight on my shoulders.

'Stay here for Vespers, Gendal. The singing of our evening office will give God space to refresh you. May He grant you the answers you seek.'

Brother Matthias walked back into the darkness, leaving me alone there. After a little time, a small congregation of local people gathered around me. To help my reflections while I waited for the service, I opened the mirror locket I always carried. It reminded me of Arzandel, the wizard of fate who had guided me in my youthful quest to save the other-worldly land of Berren. Each attempt to focus on the mirror failed. My mind churned over all that I had discovered, stirred by my resentment at Arnulf's false accusation, from which God had protected me through my ploy to avoid Aglé's attentions.

The white-robed monks emerged from their cloisters to sing the office of Vespers. Their haunting plainchant calmed my clamouring thoughts by leading me beyond my situation to meditate on God's power and beauty. The monks' blended voices sang with sacred timelessness. Their holy chants washed my mind and soul clean of all the tainting grubbiness from my prolonged contact with the world. My mind cleared as I heard the repetition of the haunting antiphon they sang to mark the Fourth Sunday of Advent:

'*O Emmanuel, Rex et legifer noster, exspectatio gentium, et Salvator earum: veni ad salvandum nos Domine Deus noster.*'

'O Emmanuel, our King and Law Maker, the Hope of the nations and their Saviour, come to save us, Lord our God.'

It was as if I looked down at the problem from God's perspective, as upon a little world removed from me. The compassion in our Saviour Christ's eyes turned to sorrow at the sorry state of some. I held my breath as more of the pieces fitted into place, and I saw the plot to discredit Sigmund for what it really was.

Chapter 15
The Christmas Eve Masque

Christmas Eve started with the household cavalry's usual ride to exercise the horses. The day was fresh and a little above freezing. The darkening cloudy skies threatened snowfalls later in the day.

By the time we returned from our ride, the holiday revelry had already begun around the castle and the grounds. Indoor games such as pegs, dice, backgammon, marbles and chess had started in the Great Hall, while outside on the training field, the hardier people competed in archery, bowls, quoits and hammer throwing. I tried my luck at each, taking care always to avoid Lord Arnulf, and lost more challenges than I won. Most of the games I lost were to children because I was not minded to win.

Our main meal of the day started earlier than usual, at sundown, to enable the kitchen servants to join in the festivities too once their chores were done. We feasted well on venison, goose and salted fish, with beans, turnips, parsnips and onions, and frumenty, a sweet dish made with eggs, milk, wheat, currants and the precious spice cinnamon. As always, the local wine flowed freely among the guests. I kept to sage water, which refreshed the palate between courses as well as it kept my head clear. Across the hall, Aglé continued to watch me with adoring eyes, while I studiously ignored her. On the odd occasion when our eyes accidentally met, she blushed deeply.

As the serious business of eating drew to a close, Oscar's musicians started playing in the gallery above the hall. Their repertoire for that part of the evening was based on local folk songs. Around the hall, soft voices joined in as they played.

Once the servants had cleared most of the dishes away and moved the tables to the sides of the hall, their duties were done and they were free to join the rest of their colleagues at the far end of the hall. On the top table, Princess Eleanore graced us with her unexpected presence for the revelries. She sat with her husband Oscar on her right and her lady-in-waiting on her left. To accommodate the two ladies, Klaus and I volunteered to take our seats with the household cavalry below the dais again.

In came the mummers, dressed in colourful masked costumes to perform Act One of the local version of the Paradise Play. Adam and Eve bowed to the audience before their entertainment began. They wore skin-coloured costumes decorated with leaves, and strolled across the floor, stroking the heads of people dressed as wild animals to show the paradise of Eden. I spotted a lion, a wolf, a boar, and a bird man I thought might be a stork.

An actor dressed as a tree sidled across to Adam and Eve. Behind the tree came a man in black with the horns of a devil and a long, serpent-like tail. He took an apple from a hand in the tree and offered it to Eve. She refused twice, but accepted it when he whispered in her ear. After appearing to bite the apple, she offered it to Adam, who also refused twice before accepting the apple and biting into it too. God entered the stage, dressed in a white robe with a hem of cloud. He threw down a wooden lightning bolt and ordered Adam and Eve out of Eden. They left the stage weeping. The other characters followed them off to the sound of applause.

The musicians played more folk songs and some carols as we waited for Act Two. Guests poured freely from the jugs of local wine. Several of the men around me sang with great enthusiasm when they heard tunes they recognised. They encouraged the rest of us to join in too. The music stopped when God came back into the hall. He signalled the start of Act Two by dropping an empty tray on the flagstone by the doors.

Mary entered through the doors. She was played by the woman who had been Eve, and wore a more becoming red shift dress and a blue cloak. As she knelt in the centre of the stage, God sent Angel Gabriel over from the door to speak to her. Gabriel wore a white robe with magnificent wings. The wings were attached to his arms and hampered him as he mimed God's message about giving Eve a baby. Eve nodded vigorously to show us all that she agreed to abide by God's will. Gabriel raised his wings to hide her, to symbolise the Holy Spirit overshadowing her. Then the angel went off and Joseph, the former Adam, came on leading a real donkey. Mary turned her back to us and turned forward again, looking pregnant.

The inn keeper entered carrying a lantern, and scattered straw on a part of the floor. He mimed telling Joseph and Mary there was no room at the inn and pointed to the straw to symbolise his stable. As they settled with the donkey in the stable, Gabriel entered with two more angels, and the musicians played and sang a carol based on the words *Gloria in excelsis Deo, et in terra pax hominibus bonae voluntatis*: Glory to God in the highest, and on earth peace to all men of good will.

The angels moved away to reveal Mary and Joseph kneeling by a crib holding a little baby. Three actors dressed as shepherds came in, one young, one adult and one old. After they had given the gift of a lamb to Joseph, three men entered dressed as Magi. The rich silks and glittering costumes of the Magi looked more ostentatious than I had expected at a travelling actors' show. I watched the Magi's masked faces closely from the side as they gave Mary their gifts of gold, frankincense and myrrh.

The actors formed a tableau group in the centre of the hall. They should then have bowed to Prince Oscar and left the hall to prepare for Act Three, Jesus' death and resurrection. Instead, one of the Magi stood up, threw off his silk cloak and tossed aside his oriental mask.

In the centre of the hall stood Prince Oscar's older brother Sigmund, tall, powerful, blond; and returned from the dead.

'Rehlein!' I gasped, leaping to my feet in shock and joy.

My joy turned to horror as I realised I had delivered a false message to both Oscar's court and the court of Sinter's father, Volkmar. I recalled Prince Volkmar's strange comment about Sinter and Sigmund just being in the next room, and cursed myself for assuming Volkmar's mind had gone, when I should have looked in the next room to check.

'So, Oscar, you can rejoice even at your brother's death!' Sigmund roared, striding forward to point an accusing finger at him.

Oscar leapt up in indignation to rail at his visitor, but thought twice and turned on me instead.

'Liar! What plot is this, that you stab your host in the back for our generosity?'

'Pray believe me, your Highness: I thought I saw him dead,' I protested.

'Blame not my messenger, Oscar. Gendal only carried the message entrusted by the sender. As the recipient, you were the one to interpret it.'

'Then what is my brother's intention in this base plot, to tear my heart strings so?'

'Is your conscience so short, that I must remind you of your grosser plot, your base theft of my reputation? I return to reclaim my innocence, which your men stole from me when they accused me of our father's death.'

'But you are the murderer!' shouted Lord Opecz.

'The son who poisoned his father to inherit the title!' added Arnulf.

Suddenly the hall bristled with the daggers we had used to eat the Christmas feast, the only knives convention allowed us to bring.

'Arrest him! If he is innocent, let him prove it!' shouted Arnulf.

'Trial by combat!' Opecz said.

Oscar leapt down from the dais to face Sigmund with Arnulf and Opecz on either side of him. Fearing for my friend, I jumped up onto the table and took two shields down from the wall display for protection. I leapt back down and pushed through the jostling crowd to Sigmund's side.

The two brothers were pressing their daggers against each other's chest. They glared in sibling rage, their faces just inches apart. With so little space between them, I shoved the two shields in the gap and forced them apart before either could do the other harm.

'Stop!' I commanded in a voice loud enough for all to hear as I forced them apart. I had to shout 'Stop!' again before they backed off and lowered their blades.

'What has got into you both?' I demanded. 'Would you have a

mother lose both her sons and her husband over this? Would you have a mother-to-be lose the father of her child too? Call this off until tomorrow and the cold sober light of day. Then let us put the case to our Lords, to decide if Prince Sigmund should be tried by a jury of his peers.'

In the awkward silence that followed, we could all hear Eleanore and Herlinde sobbing softly in relief.

I handed Sigmund one of the shields and dragged him out through the crowded hall to safety.

Chapter 16
Sigmund's Story

I took Sigmund to my room on the top floor of the royal apartments to hide him from the resurging uproar in the hall below. To lock us in, I pushed Goswin's couch across to block the door again, this time more for Sigmund's safety than for my reputation.

'Thank you, Gendal, for getting me out of yet another sticky situation,' he said with a broad, confident grin. 'You seem to have a habit of doing that.'

'What were you trying to achieve, Rehlein?' I demanded, shaking my head at the childish bravado of his return.

'It was Sinter's idea. Lull them into a false sense of security, and then spring upon them to see their guilt.'

I snorted in contempt. 'I might have known the idea came from your cousin. Whenever you've been with him, you change, and it's not for the better.'

'But aren't you pleased to see me alive?'

I turned away, unable to answer because of the conflicting emotions flooding my thoughts. When I found a way to voice how I felt, I turned back.

'Yes, Sigmund, I am pleased to see you alive. But I also feel very angry, very confused, and very used. Because suddenly a lot of things have been turned on their heads, and I realise how little you trusted me. You have destroyed my good reputation in trying to reclaim yours. You made me deliver a message you knew would not be true. And that is a hard wrong to forgive.'

'Oh, Gendal, Gendal! I needed you to believe that I really was dead. I could not risk letting you in on the plan, in case you accidentally let something slip.'

'You say you could not trust me? After all those miles we travelled together on the road? How many times have I betrayed you before?'

'None. You have always been a true friend and guide, Cara Gendal. But I feared you would let something slip, the way Sinter's father let slip about us being in the next room. I believed, that if you did not know, you could not betray me.'

He was trying to manipulate me with his use of the Celtic title he had addressed me by in the past, *Anam Cara* or soul friend. I could not speak for fear that my emotions would overcome my self-control and make me vent my fury, to retaliate for the hurt I felt at not being trusted, and my rage at his contempt for my integrity.

He saw my displeasure and spoke on.

'I knew that when you brought the news of my death here, you would realise something was not right. It is your nature to brood on such discrepancies until you ferret out a solution to satisfy your enquiring mind. I knew you would have to find out what was wrong. Was I right?'

'Yes, you were right.'

'And have you found the truth?'

'Yes, I think I have found the truth.'

'And can you tell me?'

'Yes, I could, but not yet. First, I need you to tell me what happened when your father died, as you recall it.'

'But why?' He sounded like a petulant child, trying to get out of a hated lesson.

'Precisely: why. Because what you tell me will help me understand the why as well as the what. So let's start with this. Why did you end up drinking yourself to oblivion before I came across you at the Bush Inn at Strasbourg?'

Sigmund nodded in resignation and sat down on a settle by the fire to throw on another log. He told his tale to the flames while I listened from my seat by the dressing table.

'It's a long story. It goes back to the week of the May Day holiday. My father had arranged a four day Maying feast. Oscar and I helped our father host the gathering. Sinter and his father were there, and lots of lovely young women came with their parents and chaperones. My father wanted us both to find a wife. Mother had arranged for me to partner the lovely Lady Eleanore on our Maying rides. Eleanore is pretty, and pious, and totally vacuous. I didn't want to marry a brood mare. The sort of woman I wanted as my life partner would be my friend and companion, my equal, not my possession. Like Count Bertram's Ened, or a womanly version of you.'

I thought Sigmund's assessment of Eleanore was unfair. She had struck me as being anything but vacuous.

To keep Sigmund on my side, I replied, 'This culture does not produce women of breeding like that, Sigmund. Social mores require noble women to be pure, chaste, and subservient bearers of heirs.

They are discouraged from having any independent thought.'

'That was what Father said. He told me it was time for me to marry and make heirs. He said that was why he and Volkmar had arranged the four-day feast, so that Oscar and I, and cousin Sinter, would find suitable wives.'

He stood up with his back to the fire and looked down at me. His eyes glistened as he recalled the events. I knew he was facing the truth in his own mind, even if he did not reveal it all to me.

'The day's maying was over,' he continued; 'Most of the men were handing back their horses to the stable hands in the courtyard. The women had gone to the solarium to gossip over their fancies. My father and I were left on our own in the Lesser Hall. Father said, "Lady Eleanore is a fine young woman: you could do far worse than her." I agreed she was that, but she was not for me. "Your brother Oscar is very taken with her," he said. "Then let Oscar have her," I replied. He was very angry at this. He shouted at me about the need to marry and make heirs, about my responsibility to continue the family line. Then suddenly, he stopped.'

Sigmund moved the settle to my left. He sat as he had done that May day to demonstrate with his actions what he was describing in words.

'Father looked different, somehow. The lines had vanished from the right side of his face. He was slipping down in his seat. I asked him what was wrong, and I put my arm around him to hold him up and support him.'

He placed his right arm around my shoulders in a tight grip to show me.

'Father tried to speak. The words made no sense. Then he reached for his goblet with his left hand. I realised he was trying to say *drink*, as if he was asking me for help. I picked up his goblet in my left hand and raised it to his mouth. It was full of red wine. As I tilted the goblet, wine ran out of the sides of his mouth and he choked. Then he relaxed in my arms and I tilted the goblet again. This time, the wine went down. But then people ran in, and someone dashed the goblet from my grasp. He shouted, *murderer*! I sprang back in dismay, and Father fell to the floor.'

Sigmund struggled to control the grief washing over him through being forced to relive that tragic event. I gave him time to master his emotions before gently prompting him to continue. His voice wavered as he addressed the floor.

'People lifted my father up and laid him on the table. His eyes were frightened, but nothing else could move. People dragged me away against the wall. Brother Matthias came and diagnosed apoplexy. But Lord Arnulf dismissed this, saying I had murdered him. So they forced me up to my room and locked me in for two days. Father died while I was confined. They let me out for his funeral.'

'How did people treat you at the funeral?'

'They shunned me. Some deliberately talked in my hearing about me murdering him. I realised Father might have died through what I had done, while I held him in my arms. I was desolate.'

'Was that why you started drinking heavily?'

'I had to silence the guilt in all my thoughts. Drink gave me oblivion for a few hours. But then it all came back again the next day. They made me feel an outcast: I was shunned and despised. So one day I packed my saddlebags, saddled my horse, and rode off, away from all those memories. But it didn't work. The places changed, but the memories still came with me.'

'Do you remember them talking about trial by combat before you left, or taking you to be judged by your peers in the court of

Frederick, King of Rome?'

Sigmund reflected and shook his head. 'No. I must have been too drunk to notice, let alone care.'

'So then I came across you at the Bush Inn in Strasbourg.'

'And you persuaded me to go adventuring again, as we had done when we were young fools. And I went, because you offered me a new way to find oblivion. I dared not raise my hand against my body because I would forfeit my soul. But with you I hoped to find some hopeless cause where I could end my life in some heroic deed, and die a noble death.'

'Which we found in the fight between Danuvia and Rabenwald. But you stopped seeking death.'

'You taught me well over those few short weeks. That a life lived in the service of others, can transform a hurt soul wallowing in self-pity and grief. I really came to love those mountain folk, and I detested their oppressors. Theirs was a cause worth fighting for.'

'And yet you abandoned them.'

'I didn't intend to. When I sent my begging letter to Sinter and Uncle Volkmar, they told me they thought I had been accused of a crime I did not commit. They said Oscar had hounded me out of my birth-right. They suggested a plan to fake my death and Sinter's and persuaded me to take part. I went along with it because they were the first in my family to believe in me. They made me feel so much better, I felt I had to carry out their plan.'

I recalled how changed Sigmund had looked on his return to Danuvia after visiting his cousin. His stance had been more upright, his bearing more noble: he had become a golden prince of princes.

'And yet you rode away, Sigmund. At the height of battle. And you betrayed your new friends, and me; for them: for this charade of a confrontation, which went so wrong today.'

'But it hasn't gone wrong. For now you have the answers, and we can bring the truth to light at last.'

I nodded and thought for some time. Some areas of Sigmund's testimony conflicted with what I had heard elsewhere, raising discrepancies I still needed to resolve. I questioned him again.

'The time you last spoke to your father, what was covering the floor of the room?'

'Nothing, perhaps? No, I think there were some strewn rushes. Why do you ask that?'

'When the goblet was dashed from your hand, where did it land?'

'It landed on my left. Someone backhanded it out of my grasp.'

'Did the spilt red wine react with the rushes?'

'No. It marked the table, though.'

'Do you remember who knocked the goblet from your hand?'

'An equerry? No, I was wrong – it was Lord Arnulf.'

'Did anyone help you get away?'

'My former tutor.'

'How did he do that?'

'Oh, Gendal, I tire of all these endless questions. Can't we just be done for tonight?'

'Your tiredness is nothing to the hurt I feel at the way you used me for your own ends. As you have given me the job of proving your innocence without even asking me, at least let me do it to the best of my ability until it is done.'

Sigmund's head dropped lower on his chest in the face of his guilt. He was about to respond when three knocks disturbed the silence.

The chamber door crept open until it was stopped by the couch. Someone was trying to come in.

Chapter 17
Escape

I raised my finger to my lips to warn Sigmund not to speak, and crept noiselessly over to Goswin's couch which was blocking the doorway.

'Who is that?' I hissed in a disguised voice, fearing the knock on the door meant the return of Aglé.

The caller was not fooled by the change in my voice. 'It's Goswin, Sir,' he whispered through the slight gap between the door and the jamb.

I pulled the couch aside a few inches to give him enough room to enter. Once he was inside, I blocked the door again.

Goswin saw Sigmund and faltered to a halt in the centre of the room. He bowed low before him.

'Your Highness! Everyone is looking for you. They think you left with the mummers,' he said, overawed.

'And so I should have been, page, but for that scrap. Gendal, how do we get out of here?'

'You spring the Christmas surprise of all surprises, and then expect me to rescue you?' I retorted.

'It won't be the first time,' he said with a cheeky grin.

Goswin stood with mouth agape to see his lord and master bantering with me.

My mind ran through the possibilities of escape: climbing down from the battlements by rope, brazening things out with the guards at the castle gate, seeking the help of sympathetic supporters within the castle or without. I even toyed with the idea of asking Aglé and her family for help, but shuddered at the thought of what that might cause later.

'How many entrances are there to this castle, Sigmund?' I asked.

'Two: the main gate, and a postern gate which leads from the garden down some steep steps straight into the town,' he replied. 'When I lived here last, we used to keep a key nearby to unlock the door, but it has been a long while since and it may not have been oiled.'

'Who knows of the postern?'

'Besides me? Just Oscar, I think. We used to use it when we were younger to sow our wild oats. That's how I came to be in the inn when I first met you, years ago. Our mother certainly knows of it. She keeps her key in her room as the door leads from the shed in her herb garden.'

I recalled my interview with Lady Herlinde in that same garden when I had first arrived. The main feature I had noticed in the outer wall was the row of niches holding bee skeps. I only had a vague recollection of her leaving a little shed beyond those.

'Then the postern it must be,' I said.

We discussed the layout of the castle to plan how to get to the herb garden. Goswin told us about the men at arms Oscar had sent to search for Sigmund, and where to avoid meeting the residents and guests he had instructed to stay close to the castle. His information helped me form a detailed plan in my mind. My first action was to check the lad's loyalty, as he would play an important role in our escape.

'Goswin, I want you to think carefully about what I am about to ask you. Do you want to risk everything by staying loyal to Prince Sigmund and helping us tonight? Or would you rather be safe and keep your place in this castle by staying loyal to Lord Heinrich? You are free to choose, and I will respect whichever way you decide. But if you choose Lord Heinrich, our ways must part at once, now, tonight.'

I noticed Sigmund's head jerk round on hearing his uncle's name, but he said nothing.

Goswin thought carefully. He had seen the hue and cry after Sigmund that evening, and was aware of what he might risk. After some reflection, he replied.

'Knight Gendal, Lord Heinrich has always treated me like the serf I am. He made me your page to insult you. But you have always treated me with respect. You make me feel valued. I would happily follow you into hell if that was where you said we must go. Please let me stay and help you.'

'Prince Sigmund is your witness, Goswin. Hopefully, we won't need to go as far as hell this time. Once this year was enough for me.'

I outlined my plan. As we discussed the details, Sigmund and Goswin helped me improve it through their greater knowledge of the castle and its occupants.

We sent Goswin out to bring us a coil of rope from the stables, and a dark winter cloak with a hood for Sigmund to conceal his identity. After Goswin had come back with these items, we sent him to the stables to saddle three horses. He took most of my few possessions with him.

I had swapped my court robes for my leather gambeson and mail in case of trouble. Underneath my black cloak, I carried the length of rope across my chest, from my right shoulder to my left hip. Despite my armour, I felt vulnerable with only a dagger for a weapon, the knife I had used at the Christmas Eve feast.

When the time came to move, Sigmund and I stepped noiselessly along the passage and down the stone spiral staircase past the royal apartments. We took the door into the disused Lesser Hall and crossed it in darkness. When we emerged outside, our eyes were briefly blinded by the light of the courtyard torches. Sigmund led the way to the herb garden, sneaking round the stone walls with his back against them to stay in the shadows. His quiet sure-footedness told me he had often used this route in the past. We slipped round a corner of the wall and moved out of the flaming torchlight into darkness again. After edging our way cautiously round another corner, we moved back out into light, the cold beams of the near full moon We flitted swiftly across the courtyard to the arched garden gate.

The tall gate squeaked as Sigmund pushed it open.

'We used to keep this well-oiled in the past,' he whispered, and I could hear the grin in his voice.

'Shush!' I warned, my voice even quieter than his.

We slipped through the vegetable plot into the fruit trees and paused to listen for any danger. When all seemed safe, we left the trees and entered the herb garden. We wove between the herb beds and passed the bee skeps to reach the squat stone lean-to shed built against the outer wall.

Sigmund tried the door. It opened with a loud scrape. Fearing discovery, I scanned the garden and the castle for danger. Nothing moved. I wondered whether Princess Eleanore was back at her high window even now, watching us.

Sigmund entered and tried the postern door at the back of the shed. It was firmly locked. While I checked the door for any securing bars or bolts, Sigmund felt with his fingers between the rafters above the side walls searching for the key. His foot kicked over some clay pots. They clattered to the floor. Then something small fell down, striking a broken pot with a metallic thud.

'That was the key!' he hissed. His impatience with himself for dropping it felt almost tangible in the tense atmosphere.

I returned to the garden door to keep watch while Sigmund scrabbled around the floor, looking for the key. Despite all the noise he had made, nothing stirred in the moonlit garden. The cold felt intense. My breath fogged the still air, silvered by the moonlight.

Sigmund's stifled cry of triumph announced when he had finally found the key. He felt his way back to the postern door, put the key in the lock and tried to turn it. It did not move.

'Let's use the rope to go over the wall instead,' I said.

'No need. There's always a phial of oil stored in here, for just this situation.'

I despaired of ever escaping from the shed and the castle before we were caught.

Meanwhile, as we struggled to open the postern door, Goswin was saddling up three horses in the stables: my Finstar and two hacks which were kept by the castle for general use. Goswin divided my possessions between the three saddles to hide the fact that he would be leaving with all my baggage. He rode out of the stable on one of the hacks, guiding Finstar and the other hack on lead reins, one on either side of his horse.

The castle's main gate opened as Goswin approached. His heart leapt with fear as he saw Klaus ride in. He held his nerve and waited for Klaus to clear the gate before he tried to leave.

'Halt! Where are you going?' demanded the gatekeeper.

'They asked me to bring fresh horses, sir,' Goswin replied, trying to keep the waver out of his voice.

'I didn't see you come through before.'

We had timed Goswin's departure with the horses to happen

soon after the change of guard at midnight. Goswin feared we had got the timing wrong, but responded as best he could.

'Sorry, sir. It took me longer to saddle up than it should. Please don't keep me even longer. They are waiting.'

The panic in his voice would have been appropriate for a page expecting to be beaten for taking too much time. Klaus took his part.

'They are still waiting for you down by the church, page. Don't dawdle!'

His order was enough to persuade the gatekeeper to let Goswin through. The page rode off with the three horses, down the hill towards the centre of town.

Meanwhile, we were still wrestling with the lock. Sigmund finally found the phial of oil. He poured some on the shank of the key, letting it flow down over the collar onto the bit and the wards. Then he inserted the oiled key into the lock and tried to move the mechanism inside. At first it did not respond, but after several more tries, the key reluctantly turned. Sigmund pulled the door open, and we stepped outside.

'Hah! We've got you!' shouted a man to my right. I knew his voice: he was a member of the household cavalry.

Hands grasped our upper arms and tried to push us back through the doorway into the garden. I spun round and kneed the man who clutched me. He released me and doubled up, leaving the back of his mail-covered neck exposed. I struck a sharp blow to his nape. He dropped to the ground.

Sigmund was wrestling with his assailant. I caught the man's neck in the crook of my arm and pulled sharply backwards. He fell to the ground with his head at an odd angle to his shoulders. His body tumbled from the steps and rolled away down the steep hillside.

'Thanks, Gendal,' Sigmund whispered.

He locked the postern gate behind us and pocketed the key.

We padded down the steep stone steps into the city and glided through the shadows to the inn where we had first met. We had made it our meeting point because people regularly came and went there even in the middle of the night. But now it was well after midnight and even the inn seemed eerily quiet. The moonlit streets were empty. Most people had gone to their beds.

After what felt like a long time waiting, we heard the clatter of horses' hooves on the cobbles, coming towards us. The noise sounded deafening. We hid away in a dark corner until the travellers came into view. When we saw the shadowy forms of three horses with just one rider, we came out to meet them.

Finstar whinnied to me in greeting. I hugged his neck and hoisted myself into his saddle. After Sigmund mounted the other horse, Goswin passed us our lead reins. Sigmund led the way down the hill towards the nearest city gate.

Halfway down the street, a horseman rode out of the shadows. Fear tightened my chest.

'Fear not: I mean you no harm,' he whispered. It was the voice of Knight Klaus.

'What are you doing here?' I demanded.

'No time to talk now. They will suspect a party of four less than they would two or three.'

He was right, of course, but I still did not know whether I could trust him. I feared a trap or ambush behind every turning off the road.

Klaus paired up with Sigmund as we rode on down the hill. Goswin and I rode behind them. When we reached the city gate, I expected the gatekeeper to stop our party and turn us back.

'Open the gate, Jan: the Castellan needs us,' Klaus shouted.

The gatekeeper obeyed without a word. Much to my surprise, he opened the gate and let us through. We rode on into the night, on the monastery road before turning off down a narrow back lane. Sigmund told us this was a shortcut to his castle.

'Goswin, ride closer to your horse's withers when you can't see ahead, in case there are low branches you can't see,' I warned.

'That shouldn't be a problem,' Sigmund said; 'Dietl always keeps this road clear for Dr Petrus. He buys his paper and inks from the monks.'

As we rode on along the narrow lane, clouds rolled in, obscuring the moon. The night became much darker. Large flakes of snow began to fall.

'I don't think our good doctor will be coming by this way for a few days,' Sigmund joked.

'We cannot risk riding much further tonight,' Klaus warned.

'Let's double back to the monastery,' I said.

'That is where they would expect us to go,' Sigmund said: 'Don't worry: almost all this track is sheltered by trees.'

'So sheltered, I can't even see my own legs!' I retorted.

'Where did the mummers go?' Klaus asked.

'Back to their homes, I expect,' Sigmund replied. His manner had returned to that insouciance I had previously associated with the influence of his cousin Sinter. It felt as if the whole escapade had become some sort of laddish prank.

'You endangered their lives as well as our own,' I said.

'Stop complaining! I had enough of that in your chamber.'

I fell silent at Sigmund's rebuke and followed blindly along the narrow lane. Beside me, Goswin called out with a weak and trembling voice.

'I'm very cold. I don't think I can ride much further.

I took off a riding glove and reached across to feel his hand. His bare fingers felt as cold as ice.

'Sigmund, we must stop and help the page.'

'He said he would follow us to hell.'

'Then you go on ahead. We will follow when we are able.'

My threat unsettled Sigmund enough to stop. He chatted with Klaus on horseback while I dismounted and lifted Goswin out of his saddle. The lad's clothes were pitifully thin against the winter cold. I wrapped him in Finstar's horse blanket and rubbed his hands and feet to restore the circulation. He was getting drowsy with exposure. Realising he would not be safe to ride alone, I lifted him up onto Finstar's saddle and handed the reins of his horse to Klaus. Then I wrapped myself around the lad to shelter him from the worst of the cold.

We set off again along the night-dark track. Snow was still falling where the trees did not cover us. It settled on our horses' manes and our cloaks. My doubts crept in: worry that whether Sigmund had taken us in the wrong direction, and fears for Goswin's life.

After a length of time which felt like hours, the path broadened out. We rounded the corner of a hillside and gazed across a dark valley obscured by swirling snow. On the far side stood a shadowy castle, its battlements lit by four brazier beacons. At last, Rehschloss was in sight. My flagging spirits soared.

'We're nearly there, Goswin. Keep holding on,' I told the cold young lad cradled in my arms.

He did not answer. He was totally unresponsive.

The snow fell more heavily, blotting out the view of safety only moments after we had seen its promise. We battled on through the blizzard, behind Sigmund and Klaus, down the snow-banked road towards the sleeping village and the castle beyond.

Chapter 18
An Insult Too Far

The watch had seen and heard our approach as we toiled through the snowy village and up the cobbled hill to Rehschloss castle. The gates swung open to admit us before we had crossed the causeway. Fiery torches lit the courtyard beyond the gates. We brought our horses to a halt by the steps to the Great Hall, all of us shivering, wet and doubled over our saddles with the cold. Caring hands lifted Goswin down from my lap and rushed him away to the shelter of the Lesser Hall. Sigmund, Klaus and I dismounted, our arms and legs numb. We left the stable hands to care for our horses while we followed Goswin into the hall.

Torches blazed in the wall sconces, and a large fire was burning in the hearth to warm the hall for our arrival. In the flaming torch light stood Sinter Schwarzenberg, Sigmund's second cousin, proud and haughty as always, with dark flashing eyes and a mane of black curls. Sigmund cast off his cloak and the cousins hugged.

'We had begun to doubt you, Rehlein!' Sinter teased.

'I didn't expect such problems with the lock,' Sigmund replied.

'Why didn't you tell me you had already planned this?' I asked.

'You were being tiresome. Gendal. I needed to make sure Oscar's men had left the courtyard. You filled that time for me by adding the final touches to our plan.'

Kitchen maids brought us bread and some hearty hare and vegetable soup, which they ladled from a steaming pan into earthenware bowls. Ignoring etiquette, I sat down at the table to tuck in, listening to the others as I ate. At first, I could barely hold my spoon, but the warmth of the fire soon worked its wonders on my stiff joints. My hands and feet tingled and reddened as they thawed. I felt surprised that Sigmund and Klaus did not appear to have suffered the consequences of our journey so badly. They seemed to be buoyed up by an aura of success.

Sinter hugged Klaus with the same enthusiasm he had hugged Sigmund. They clapped each other's shoulders, as though they had executed some challenging stratagem with confident success.

'Well done, Klaus! You were right to warn us!' Sinter said.

'Then it was true?' the young knight asked in reply.

'I didn't realise you knew Sinter too, Klaus!' I said, forgetting our reception at Schwarzenberg.

'Another second cousin,' Sinter said with a smirk.

Klaus joined me at the table and drew over a bowl of the warming soup. He explained:

'Prince Volkmar asked me to look out for you, Gendal, long before we met. When you arrived at Harzberg, you asked a lot of questions about Umbert. I could see you were setting yourself up for trouble. But I didn't expect it to happen so soon. After they attacked you on the training field, I made sure I kept nearby.'

'I didn't make things easy for you, Klaus. You seemed too good to be true. Were you responsible for the ghost at Rehschloss?'

He frowned with a lack of comprehension and supped some of the soup. I pressed my point with him.

'The false ghost struck a few hours after you delivered Prince Oscar's invitation to the Solstice celebrations. Did you make the tower in the bedroom above me? – with stolen pots and pans and snow, balanced to crash down the middle of the night?'

Sinter and Sigmund laughed.

'Not that old prank!' Sigmund said. He took his place at the head of the table to eat some bread and soup with us.

Klaus dropped his head.

'I didn't think,' he admitted. The squire who came with me asked if it was really possible. He'd heard how Sigmund had played the prank on Dr Petrus years ago. As we had nothing much to do that afternoon, I used the time to show him.'

'That was my idea originally,' Sinter bragged, joining us at the table. 'I love the way pivots work. I never tire of fulcrums, balances, trebuchets and the like. When I stayed here once, Petrus was happy to teach me all about them. We paid him back with a demonstration!'

Sigmund laughed. 'Oscar and I tried it again a few times after that, but we always got caught before we could make it work.'

Having lessened the pressure on Klaus, Sinter changed the subject back to our more immediate concerns.

'Yes, Klaus, your warning had proved correct. I sent a cohort along the riverside road tonight. They confirmed some men had blocked the highway at the narrows.'

'Was it an ambush?' Sigmund asked.

'Probably. The six were dressed as vagabonds, so we cannot be sure who was responsible.'

'I hadn't heard anything like that in the barracks, only an aside at the table,' Klaus said. 'Is that why we took the back road, Sigmund?'

'It was,' he agreed. 'It's always been a useful track for us.'

He reminisced further, recounting several stories about the times he and Sinter had used the back road to evade the watchful eyes of parents and tutors. Sinter joined in and regaled us with more tales of youthful escapades linked to that track.

Their laddish banter fanned the flames of the resentment which had been smouldering in my thoughts ever since Sigmund had unmasked himself at Harzberg. How could these princes laugh and joke without a care when their deeds had taken Goswin to death's door with exposure, and left my integrity in ruins? The resentment grew too loud for me to leave my thoughts unsaid. I crashed into their conversation, interrupting the raillery.

'Enough of this! Prince Sinter, I have a bone to pick with you.'

As the words came out of my mouth I realised the seriousness of my social gaffe, and only then thought of its consequences.

'I am not accountable to a ministerialis!' Sinter stated, pronouncing my title as a putdown to keep me in my place.

I ignored his slight, having spoken truth in the past even to the Imperator. With the damage already done, I challenged him in return, knowing I could not make my situation any worse.

'Your Highness, were you the master planner responsible for tonight's escapade?'

Sinter was too proud of his achievements to see the trap I was setting him.

'I was.'

'And were you also the creator of the cowardly plan to run away in the height of battle at Dernfels, leaving your allies fatally weakened?'

Sinter frowned in surprise to hear my raking up that part of their past exploits, despite all the other past deeds he and Sigmund had referred to that night.

'As if Sigmund and I should have risked our lives for that crowd of mountain peasants!'

'That was the battle where I nearly died. Then where would your plans have been?'

'But you can't die. You've been to fairyland.'

'Fairyland?' I repeated, appalled.

Memories flooded back from my childhood of being branded a changeling because my body had not developed quite like those of other children. My village had blamed two years' poor harvests on me for bringing bad luck. Under pressure from their neighbours, my parents had sold me to a passing stranger, and I never saw them again.

I strove to mask my bitter memories behind a wooden face so that I could focus on Sinter's impatient reply.

'All right: Halsanger, Berren, wherever it was Rehlein told me. The bloody hall in the land of tombs,' he said.

'And that justifies your craven act of running away and leaving us to our fate?'

His eyes darkened at being called a coward for a second time that night.

'It was necessary. We needed Oscar to think his brother was dead. Rehlein told me you would realise something was wrong when you gave Oscar the letter. So you would stay to investigate. Which you did.'

His arrogant complacency sickened me. To avoid insulting the prince further with my words, I left the table and turned my back on him to go to Goswin, insulting him instead with my actions.

The lad was lying awake in a cocoon of blankets by the fire, tended by a young nursemaid. He gave me a weak smile. His wan face looked golden in the light of the flaming logs blazing in the fire basket.

'I'm glad to see you're awake again, Goswin.' I patted his shoulder. 'Next time, let me know sooner when you're struggling.'

'But I let you down, Sir; I held you back,' he said with tears in his eyes.

'The only people who let me down are the ones who dreamed up their foolish plan and didn't prepare us well enough for it.'

I looked across at Sigmund, who saw my expression and at least had the grace to look discomforted. Encouraged, I returned to the table and stayed standing to watch the princes as I forced them to face the full consequences of their deeds.

'So Sigmund, you sent your begging letter to Schwarzenberg, saying, what? Please send me 500 gold pieces. I want to help pay off a Condottiero for Count Bertram of Rabenberg, who I've allied myself with against the Duke of Danuvia?'

'It wasn't put that way, but that was the essence,' Sigmund said.

'And Prince Volkmar received it, and sent you, Sinter, with the money, knowing this estate would repay you the same way it had repaid you for clearing Sigmund's drinking debts?'

Sinter's eyes flashed with barely concealed fury at my holding him to account. 'We understood why Sigmund had been drinking. We realised he was about to kill himself honourably in some futile battle, all because he had been unjustly condemned as his father's murderer. So my father sent me with the money, and an escort of five hundred cavalry to rescue Rehlein whichever way we could.'

I recalled overhearing a conversation between the two cousins in the command pavilion, two days before the battle of Dernfels. Sinter had said, *Are you fool enough to risk even your life for this paltry mountain?* I had not understood his words then. Now it was clear he had been persuading Sigmund to abandon his death wish and reclaim his family's honour and his lost inheritance. When Sigmund had told Sinter the generals thought him a coward, he must have asked the generals for fighters to exchange surcoats, helmets and shields with them.

'So on the day of the battle, you both swapped clothes with two of the foot soldiers,' I pressed; 'And while they were dying in the melee, you two rode off with your five hundred cavalrymen, leaving the back of the hill undefended, and almost losing us the battle before it had even begun?'

Sinter's head was down. He had given up trying to defend himself and would have blocked his ears if he could. His resentful expression told me he had rarely been made accountable for his deeds before. In comparison, Sigmund looked chastened, with his shoulders slumped and his head down. He had always dreamed of heroic glory and felt ashamed to discover just how unheroic his actions had been.

I continued, on weaker ground as I was now surmising events. 'So your company came back to Schwarzenberg. There you worked out the final details of your plan and waited for me to take the news of your deaths to Prince Oscar.'

Sigmund nodded. 'But you never came. We wondered whether you had perished in the November floods. What took you so long?'

His petulant criticism served only to stoke my fury.

'What took me so long? I nearly died of my wounds following that battle. Duke Nicolaus took me prisoner and kept me in a windowless storage cell for weeks. When he released me, he tried to have me assassinated. Then he finally tried to dispatch me himself with a cohort of guards and mercenaries at Danbrucke. If not for Count Erhart's actions, Count Bertram and I would not have lived to tell the tale.'

'See, I told you Gendal is protected by the fairies,' Sinter crowed.

'It is my God who protects me: not fairies, or witches or magic amulets. My integrity is my most precious possession. Which you two callously destroyed when you sent me to deliver a message you knew would not be true. I've had enough of the lot of you. You can finish this yourselves, without me. I'm done!'

I marched out of the hall in rage. Klaus rose from the table to chase after me. Sinter stopped him

'No, Klaus,' Sigmund warned; 'Let Gendal be.'

Chapter 19
Christmas Day

After our late night escapade, I woke about noon on Christmas Day. At first, I wondered where I was as the low attic ceiling seemed unfamiliar. Then memories of the night before flooded back: the journey, the argument, and being demoted to sleep in one of the nursery rooms because worthier guests already occupied the state bedrooms. My head was heavy with an emotional hangover intensified by poor sleep, which felt as debilitating to me as any hangover caused by wine. Pounding regrets warned me that my tirade against Sinter and Sigmund had just made my difficult situation even more perilous.

Across the room came the sound of soft breathing. Goswin lay asleep in a cot, the cares gone from his face. His ruddy complexion told me he had recovered from the privations of the snowy ride the night before, for which I gave thanks to God.

Outside, below our window, a mounted escort of twenty-five soldiers was about to leave the courtyard. They wore chain mail covered with the white surcoat of the yellow Schwarzenberg sun on their chests and warm cloaks on their backs. They were well armed with swords and spears and bucklers. In their centre rode Prince

Sinter and his father Prince Volkmar with Sinter's mother Ilse between them, the lady I had met during my visit to Schwarzenberg Castle. Volkmar had wrapped himself in furs for protection from the cold. Ilse straddled her horse like the men around her, the skirts of her green winter gown ample enough to stretch over the saddle and cover her legs to the ankle of her leather riding boots. She was fastening a heavy brown wool cloak and hood around her shoulders as I watched, to give herself extra warmth on the journey.

Behind them rode Klaus, looking bright enough despite his Christmas Eve adventures. His youth must have helped compensate for his lack of sleep. Behind him trailed five luggage horses, marshalled by some of the soldiers at the rear of the party. The quantity of luggage and the timing of their departure suggested they were travelling to Harzberg to join Oscar for his Christmas celebrations.

The convoy rode out through the gates of Rehschloss with a flourish of trumpets and a clatter of horses' hooves. Behind me, Goswin woke and yawned and stretched. I turned back to him.

'How are you today, Goswin?'

'I'm sorry, Sir. I've slept in,' he said, struggling to rise.

'It's Christmas Day. You are allowed to sleep in today, especially after our adventures last night. We are safe in Rehschloss. Sleep on if you feel you need to.'

He lay back and his eyelids closed. Soon his regular breathing told me he had fallen back asleep.

I wandered down to the kitchen block to find some food and the makings for a herbal tea. The cooks and their assistants fell silent when I entered the warm stuffy main kitchen. Though I feared I had alienated them too, they provided what I wanted readily enough. When I left the kitchen with a plate of bread and cheese and a warm drink, their voices started up again, suggesting I had been the subject of their gossip.

I took my simple meal to the library to eat in peace. Dr Petrus sitting there as usual, reading a book by the fire. As always, he was dressed in his long black scholastic robes and four pointed hat.

He looked up at me with a kindly expression. His chin dropped and his eyebrows arched in that timeless teacher's look of enquiry.

'Welcome, Gendal. You have slept well, despite your late night?'

'Enough, thank you, Doctor. I hope our late arrival didn't disturb you too much.'

He laughed. 'You could not have prevented that. The whole castle heard your debate. Was it wise to make yourself an enemy of Prince Sinter? He is a powerful man.'

I shook my head and wiped my face to conceal the depth of my chagrin. Then I tore off a morsel of bread with such force I crushed it between my fingers.

'No, it was not wise. But his arrogance! His contempt! His insults! They were too much to stomach after he had abused my trust.'

'When you reacted as you did, you gave him power over your emotions. Yet usually you are a calm and rational being. Why do you think that happened?'

I considered the question carefully. At first I blamed Sinter, for his manipulation of me for his own ends, as if I were a pawn being played without conscience on the chessboard of his strategy. But I had learned some time ago, that it was not the events themselves which disturbed my equilibrium, but my interpretation of those events. Normally I would have responded with equanimity, controlling my emotions in order to outplay my rival; a quality which had helped my promotion to ministerialis. But that night my reactions had been the reverse, fuelled totally by overwhelming emotions of hurt pride and umbrage at injustice. I came to see how my physical circumstances had seriously influenced my judgement, for the worse.

'I was hungry,' I admitted; 'I was angry. I felt insulted and abused. And I felt intensely tired.'

'Would you react the same way now, had that conversation been held this morning rather than last night?'

A part of me marvelled at his excellent teaching technique, even as he made me face up to the shame of my situation. My focusing on his skill rather than my folly helped to lessen the sting of the kindly reprimand he was giving me.

'No,' I confessed. My voice was almost inaudible.

'What was that?' he asked.

I repeated my answer more clearly.

He smiled to encourage me. 'Good. We now know why that happened. What do you think you can do about it?'

My head was still too foggy with the aftermath of extreme emotion to sift through it all for a solution.

'I don't know – nothing, I suspect. As I've quit, I'll have to leave here; find somewhere else for the winter. Before I go, I will need to make arrangements for Goswin. None of this has been his fault.'

'But you have not completed your commission, the task Sinter and Sigmund set you to do.'

'I don't understand,' I said, trying to hide the fact that I understood all too well.

Petrus gave me that questioning look again. It penetrated through my defensiveness and told me he saw through my lie.

'Gendal, you have not yet told anyone what your findings are.

That has already placed you in great danger. Was Sigmund guilty of murder? Or did others have designs against him? You need to reveal the truth before someone tries again to stop you. Because next time, they may well succeed.'

'I cannot tell anyone yet, Doctor Petrus. I know the answer, but I don't yet have enough proof to make the accusation.'

'Your silence places you in a very dangerous situation.'

'That I have come to realise.'

'And insulting Prince Sinter has made even Rehschloss a dangerous place to be.'

'Is that why the kitchen went silent when I went for some food?'

'The servants admire you for speaking out against Prince Sinter. But they know all too well the problems his wrath will cause you. They don't want his curse on you to rebound upon them.'

I threw myself back in my chair and wiped my face again.

'What should I do?'

'Apologise. If he will accept it.'

'What? Apologise to that manipulating manifestation of evil? Never! I meant every word I said. I will not let him off the hook, just to toady back in with him.'

Again Petrus looked up at me with that questioning expression.

'You speak as if you think forgiveness is your gift to him Pray, think again. Do you recall the *Pater Noster*, the prayer our Lord taught his disciples?'

I nodded.

He continued, 'We pray *et dimitte nobis debita nostra sicut et nos dimittimus debitoribus nostrus*. Forgive us our debts as we forgive the debts of others. We forgive others for our own sakes, not for the sakes of those who wronged us. Consider how much our good Lord has forgiven you. Do you want that debt returned?'

I recalled the parable of the unforgiving servant in Matthew's Gospel and knew the doctor was right.

'But how can I approach Prince Sinter now, Dr Petrus? He has just departed with his parents.'

'They go to Harzberg to stay for Christmas. They will send for you and Prince Sigmund to join them at court once Prince Volkmar has placated Prince Oscar.'

'That will make it even harder to approach Sinter.'

'Ask God for guidance. He will show you the way.'

Chapter 20
Sigmund's Arrest

The order to return to Oscar's court at Harzberg came three days later. Dr Petrus and I spent the intervening time enjoying each other's company in the Rehschloss library, where he drew more heraldic designs while I took pleasure in reading the few books on the shelves. It proved an excellent place to keep out of Sigmund's way. We only met once daily, for the communal evening meal in the Great Hall. I took care then to keep Petrus between us at the top table. The number of mouths fed by the castle still included the twenty-five Schwarzenberg household cavalrymen Sinter had left to protect his cousin, making the Great Hall the best place for us to eat together.

Dr Petrus and I were talking in the library when the summons arrived from Oscar.

'What circumstances brought you to this land to live and work?' I had asked Petrus, judging he knew me well enough now for me to presume upon his patience with such a question.

'Ah. I am a distant relative of Lady Herlinde and Lord Heinrich: a fifth son of a sixth son. So my heritage is great, but my inheritance was modest. Like Oscar, I have no aptitude for war, which ruled out becoming a knight. But I did have a way with letters, which opened the door to the Church.'

'With your abilities, good doctor, I am sure you would have been a cardinal by now if you had stayed. What happened?'

'I fell in love with a beautiful young woman shortly after I had graduated from Bologna, my darling Silvana. I did right by her and we married, which meant I could no longer live under holy orders. My family arranged for me to have a modest living here, teaching the Prince's children etiquette and letters.'

'I don't recall seeing your wife.'

'Sadly, Silvana died in childbirth, and so did the child. We had just two happy years together.'

'Did you try to return to the church?'

'No. All my wants are cared for here, and I have far more freedom than I would as a priest.'

As he was speaking, we heard a clatter of horses' hooves in the courtyard. We went to the window to watch Lord Arnulf ride in below us with twenty cavalrymen wearing the red on white Hart of Harzland surcoats. A squire came out to hold Arnulf's horse for him to dismount. He waved him away and remained in the saddle.

'Fetch Sigmund,' Arnulf ordered the squire. 'Sheriff Opecz has issued a warrant for him to be taken to Harzberg for examination.'

Petrus and I looked at each other in concern. We both knew Arnulf had overstepped his authority by informing the squire of his intention to arrest Sigmund. I turned towards the door. Petrus held me back.

'This will be why Prince Sinter left half his men stationed here. We do not need to involve ourselves yet.'

Down in the courtyard, Steward Dietl approached Arnulf and asked to see the warrant. Arnulf showed him the text but did not let the paper leave his hand.

'We will need to ready the horses,' Dietl said. 'As that will take a little time, I invite you to dismount and have some food in the Great Hall while we get everything ready.'

'Don't take all day about it. I have orders to bring him to Harzberg before nightfall.'

The company of riders dismounted on Arnulf's signal. Goswin was among the pages who came out to take their horses to the stables, freeing them to go to the Great Hall.

We turned as the library door swung open behind us. Sigmund came in.

'Gendal, I need you to come with me,' he said.

I was about to remind him I had quit his service when Petrus silenced me with that questioning glare he loved to use.

'If I help you counter these charges, I would expect your help in handling Prince Sinter,' I replied.

'Of course,' he said without thinking.

'Then I shall go and pack.'

We went our separate ways and met up again on the steps of the Lesser Hall as our pages brought out our horses. Sigmund's horse carried little baggage, whereas Finstar was carrying all my few possessions in my saddlebags. The courtyard thronged with mounted household cavalry. Arnulf's twenty men of Harzland were more than matched by twenty-five of Volkmar's knights. As we mounted up, Sigmund gave me a boyish smile.

'We have foiled them by kindness!' he said, and rode off to join

Arnulf. Puzzled by his remark, I instructed Goswin to stay at Rehschloss for his safety and fell in behind the Lord and the Prince.

Our column rode out of the castle in pairs: each hart surcoat matched by the sun surcoat of Schwarzenberg. I was near the back, with one of the unmatched sun knights, the other four ahead and behind me. Wary of their intentions, I kept one hand on the pommel of the sword in my saddle scabbard while my other hand controlled Finstar's reins.

We rode for a couple of hours without incident. Our route was through the forest rather than along the river. This surprised me as the river road would be easier for such a large company.

Some of the horses at the head of the column became skittish and harder to handle for their strangely lethargic riders. As more horses and riders succumbed, I realised what Sigmund's cryptic comment had meant. His kitchen had overfed the knights to make them less responsive, while the stables had fed their horses oats to make them frisky. With Sigmund's measures and Sinter's escort, I no longer feared an unexpected attack from Arnulf's men.

We still had some way to go when I noticed a shadowy figure in the trees ahead. It was one of Silvio's men of the woods. Such outlaws were skilful enough in field craft not to be seen unless they chose to be. I wondered what had made this John of the Woods reveal his presence.

'I need to stop and check my horse. There could be a stone in his shoe,' I said to the knights around me, and leapt off Finstar, dropping his reins.

My escort of five halted while I ran my hand down Finstar's fetlocks and inspected his hooves in apparent concern. Satisfied that all was fine, I handed over Finstar's reins, made a second excuse and slipped off into the undergrowth.

I hid among the bushes several feet away from the road. A wild man dropped from the trees above and landed in front of me. He wore mostly fur to cover his short, stocky body. He had not combed his fuzzy red hair for many years, and his skin was filthy.

'Silvio sent me. There's an ambush ahead,' he warned, and disappeared into the undergrowth before I could reply.

The content of his warning came as no surprise, but I did wonder why the woodmen thought to warn me when I was travelling in a well-armed column of trained cavalry. I had always tried to keep on the right side of the wild men of the woods for my personal safety, but did not consider them my allies.

I returned to my escort of and remounted Finstar. We set off at a brisk trot to catch up with the main column. We turned the next corner, to find the road ahead blocked by a melee. Forty mounted horsemen were crushed together in a small clearing, fighting eight unmounted roughnecks dressed in sacking cloaks and hoods.

My escort of five abandoned me to wade into the fray. I stayed back, glad to have been forgotten.

The cavalrymen flashed their swords and spears with great energy, but they made little contact with their adversaries. The roughnecks used their bucklers to advantage but did little more than brandish their knives and swords. The entire scene looked like one of those spectacles put on by royal courts to entertain the ladies.

I looked more carefully and noticed how well-polished the roughnecks' leather footwear was. Nor were their weapons the cheap knife-blade swords used by the common people. They appeared to be working in collusion with the Harzberg horsemen, fighting against the Schwarzenberg horsemen. These men had surrounded Prince Sigmund and were protecting him from the fray.

It seemed the perfect opportunity to abscond from the company, especially when neither the Schwarzenberg nor the Harzberg knights had any interest in keeping me alive, and possibly had instructions to cause my death in this bizarre charade. I turned Finstar's head and trotted back round the corner. Once out of their sight, I urged Finstar into a gallop to put some distance between us and the strange scene.

Knowing I was still in danger while ron the broad road we had come by, I turned Finstar down the next track leading into the depths of the forest. We took further forks in the track, some little more than animal trails. Though I tried to take mental note of the turnings we took, I soon became lost in the dense forest. The lengthening shadows of late afternoon made it even harder to find my way between the close-growing trees.

With dusk nearing, I dismounted in a sheltered glade to rest for the night. As I undid the buckles on my baggage, a thud sounded behind me. I spun round, my dagger in my hand.

Chapter 21
A Plea for Help

I turned to find John of the Woods behind me: the wild man who had warned me about the ambush on the road.

'My apologies,' I said, and put my dagger away. If he had wanted me dead, he would have killed me already.

He smiled, put his grubby finger to his hairy lips in an instruction to keep quiet, and beckoned me to follow him. I refastened the buckles on my baggage, picked up Finstar's reins, and walked off after my unexpected guide.

He moved swiftly through the trees, so fast I found it hard to keep up with him while leading a horse encumbered by baggage. When dusk fell, our journey continued by the light of the full moon, where it could filter through the tree canopy above.

We climbed up into the hill country behind Harzland and the river, crossing streams swollen by the meltwater from the previous snows. Our path passed between eerie granite outcrops which loomed above the undergrowth. It brought us out into a sheltered cwm valley lined by trees.

A hamlet of five makeshift huts stood around a circular fire pit near a spring in the base of the cwm. The huts had been fashioned from whatever materials were to hand: stones, branches and a thatch of heather. A group of outlaws, mostly men, warmed themselves at the fire burning in the pit. One person was turning an improvised spit to roast the remnants of a deer.

'This is Gendal,' said my guide as we joined the circle.

The men gathered around me, touching my clothes, feeling my weapons. Some went through Finstar's saddlebags, and one pulled out the goblet Eleanore had given me with a cry of delight.

'Be careful with that,' I warned; 'It was the cup that killed Prince Umbert.'

The woodsman shoved the goblet back in the saddlebag at once, fearing poison and bad luck.

The leader of the outlaws stepped forward and invited me to sit at the fire. He was a tall, muscular middle-aged man dressed in an odd assortment of clothes which he had probably acquired by theft. He looked as unkempt as the man who had led me there.

'I am Silvio,' he said with a smile, which I returned. It was customary for woodland outlaws never to tell strangers their previous identities. He introduced me to his companions, who were all called either John or Jack in various linguistic forms. Though the names came from many of the furthest reaches of the Holy Roman Empire, the accents of his gang all sounded fairly local.

'I must thank you for saving me from the ambush,' I said.

He saw me eyeing the venison in hunger and gave me some slices on an unwashed wooden plate. As I gratefully devoured the chewy meat, the men around me cut off some for themselves and ate too. They passed a flagon of ale around for everyone to drink their share. I drank from it once to show I accepted their hospitality but abstained when the flagon made the rounds again.

'You'll be wondering why we brought you here,' said Silvio.

'I am.'

'Ian, show our guest your right arm.'

The unkempt man beside him held up his right arm. I had not noticed before that it ended at his fist.

'That's what Lord Arnulf did to me,' said Ian, angrily; 'And more.'

'What more?' I asked, fearing what they might tell me next.

'He burnt down my cottage,' shouted Johan, the man who had brought me there; 'My wife and child were inside.'

'He threw me off my tenancy for not paying the rent due,' said Janek; 'But the harvest had been poor and there was nothing left.'

'He raped my daughter, the only family I had left. She killed herself,' said Hans.

'He used me when none of the ladies would have him,' said a haggard woman the others called Mary.

The tales the company told were harrowing. I listened to them all and pitied these people who had fallen outside the protection of the law because of the cruelty of that one man. What made their stories more compelling, was the fact that I had seen the damage they described when I had visited the Duke of Romfeld's lands.

When they finally came to the end of their stories of woe, I struggled to respond but knew I must.

'My heart is heavy to hear all you have told me. Why do you think Lord Arnulf did such awful things?'

'He does not see us as human,' said Johan.

'He treated us like animals,' said Mary.

'He abuses his vassals as if we're his playthings,' said big Jaan.

'But his abuses would destroy the return from his estates,' I said. 'It makes no financial sense. In ruining you, he would ruin himself.'

'He did ruin himself,' said Silvio. 'Why do you think he now serves in the court of Prince Oscar?'

I felt a knot form in my stomach to hear these base witnesses corroborate my previous suspicions.

'And Lord Opecz?' I asked.

'Two of a kind,' said Silvio.

'Just the weaker of the two,' said Jaan.

I carved some more meat from the roasted venison to give myself time to think.

'And because of this, you brought me here?' I asked.

'Someone heard him give the order to slay you in the ambush,' said Silvio. 'John over there said you had got rid of the Duke of Danuvia. We thought if we saved you, you could help us back.'

'You want me to "get rid" of Lord Arnulf, too?'

'And Lord Opecz,' said Janek.

I baulked at the prospect of such an impossible task. Yet if I refused, would I even escape their lair alive? Silvio must have read my thoughts from my expression in the firelight.

'You still move in his circles, Gendal. And you must be a sore thorn in his side for him to plot to have you killed.'

'I could just said yes and ride off back to safety in Strasbourg.'

'We know you won't,' said Silvio. 'You didn't do that at Dernfels, so we know you won't for us either.'

'This is something I cannot treat lightly. Let me think about it.'

The outlaws agreed to that and finished their meal in silence.

When we settled down for the night, they gave me a bracken-padded cot to sleep on in one of their shared houses. The following morning, we fed communally on the produce of the forest, mainly game. Throughout that day, the outlaws told me more about their pasts and the injustices they wanted me to avenge.

On my second full day there, Silvio introduced me to their respected wise woman, Irmel. She lived in a hovel about a mile from their settlement. Her body was small and bent with age and the hardships of life. She had a lined face and a frail body wrapped in the rags of clothes which hinted at a better past life. The outlaws protected her and kept her well-supplied with fuel and food, in return for her medicines and her advice when they were injured or unwell.

It surprised me to discover people like Irmel dwelling in such poverty on the border of prosperous, well-run Harzland. I gazed into her knowing grey eyes and realised she had become old before her time through living in the wilds.

'Why do you dwell in these conditions, when this land is famed for its good governance and wealth?' I asked her.

She gave a bitter little laugh, and said with a knowing nod, 'Too many pigs are feeding from the same trough.' She saw my puzzled expression and added, 'The greedy one always thrives best.'

Her comment made me adjust my focus on the puzzle Sigmund had set me. While none of Sigmund's family had appeared greedy, I saw that several people living with the family did.

'Did you hear about the way Prince Umbert died last May?' I asked her.

'I did. Clear case of apoplexy.'

'In what way?'

'The prince was angry. He was arguing with his son. Then he fell back as if he had been poleaxed. A bolt from the gods.'

'He spoke after the bolt and reached for a drink.'

'It only touched one side at first. Then the gods struck him again. As much as didn't work outside, didn't work inside either. Drowning, and helpless to stop.'

The blood drained from my face as I realised what had really killed Umbert that day. My heart went out to Sigmund, who had had to live with the consequences ever since. With some trepidation, I showed Irmel the goblet Eleanore had given me and pointed to the stains inside.

'This was the cup Sigmund gave Umbert to drink from just before he died. Was it poisoned?'

She sniffed the bowl of the goblet, dabbed the stain with a damp finger to taste it, and gave the cup back to me with a snort of contempt.

'No more poisoned than the water from this holy well!'

I thanked her and gave her a halfpenny for her time. Then I left with Silvio to return to the outlaws' settlement.

At the communal fire that night, I announced my decision to the people sharing their evening meal with me.

'Ladies and gentlemen of the forest,' I began. This evoked a great deal of mirth and merriment, as intended. I continued, 'You have asked me to avenge the wrongs done to you. You have told me what happened to you, and you have shown me the evidence you carry on your bodies. I can see you have been the victims of cruel overlords. The atrocities they committed have forced you to live on the wrong side of the law.'

I reached for the communal flagon of beer and took a swig. They saw my symbolic action and knew it meant I was on their side.

'Some years ago, I received my commission from the One who is Lord of all creation: to seek justice for the poor, to defend the oppressed and to set the captive free. I cannot refuse you.'

Several outlaws cheered. Others saw from my expression that my commitment to their cause would come at a cost for me, and stayed silent.

'Two days ago, you saved me from an ambush,' I said. 'To help you now, means that tomorrow I must go back into that same danger.'

'We can take you almost to the gates,' said Johan.

But beyond those gates was where the danger lay, I thought, recalling the attack on the training field during my first day in Harzberg. I swigged from the flagon and sent it round the circle to make my contract with everyone present. When the flagon returned to me, I took one last swig before concluding the deal with a warning.

'I cannot promise you anything: just that I will do what I can.'

Silvio hugged my shoulders.

'That is all we want.'

Chapter 22
Two Apologies

I left the outlaw camp early the following morning with my woodsman guide, Johan. He took me by indistinct tracks and secret paths through the forest, almost to the gates of Harzberg. On the way we stopped at a viewpoint to admire the landscape. Below us, the city of Harzberg nestled on the hillside above the river and spread out from the rocky outcrop of the castle. The air was dry and crisp, and scented with wood smoke curling up from the houses inside the city walls.

My guide vanished back into the forest as I rode Finstar up to the city gates. Though I could no longer see the outlaw, I knew he would be watching me from some arboreal vantage point to make sure I did go into the city.

I was wearing mail and my eagle and butterfly surcoat beneath my black winter cloak. I had fastened the cloak with the Imperator's escutcheon, a small shield bearing his coat of arms. My head was protected by a leather helm, and in my hand I carried the white wand I had last used some years before while acting as the late Imperator's herald. The wand would protect me from the schemes of people like Sinter and Arnulf, but required me to act with complete impartiality.

My arrival caused a stir in the streets of Harzberg. Runners raced up the hill ahead of me to warn the castle of my presence. Streamers and pennants decorated the streets they ran through and a spirit of festivity charged the air. I realised it must be New Year's Eve, the Festival of Sylvester, and wondered whether the timing of my arrival would help or hinder my cause.

The castle gates stood open. I rode unchallenged into the courtyard. Heinrich met me at the steps to the Great Hall as he had done the day we first met. He frowned to see the mixed messages of my insignia and considered how to greet me.

'Knight Gendal, you are here as the Imperator's Herald?' he asked in concern.

I dismounted from Finstar and let a lad take him away before replying.

'I am here under my own authority, showing the insignia of the late Imperator who first used me as a Herald. I require a meeting with all now staying here who had attended the Maying Celebration when Prince Umbert died. Instruct them to assemble in the Lesser Hall at noon. I also require Brother Matthias to attend from the white friars' monastery, and Dr Petrus from Rehschloss. Dr Petrus must bring with him his Book of Heraldry and my page Goswin.'

'But today is the Festival of Sylvester.'

'What I have come to do will be done before tonight. It should grant us all a better New Year. In the meantime, arrange for me to meet with Prince Sinter.'

Heinrich nodded and led me into the Great Hall to wait while he made the other arrangements. As I sat there, a kitchen maid brought me a warm drink to counter the cold in the hall, as no fire had been lit in the cavernous fireplace yet. I had just finished the drink when Heinrich returned and instructed me to follow him. He took me up to the royal apartments and knocked at the door of one of the main guest chambers.

'Your Highness, Knight Gendal,' he announced, opening the door for me. After I had entered the warm room, he closed the door behind me.

Prince Sinter was sitting by the fire, a sneer of disdain across his haughty face. I bowed to him and waited for his permission to speak. He tried to discomfort me by taking his time to eye me up and down. But though I knew he could be a dangerous man, he was not my master. I ignored his posturing with aplomb.

'You asked to see me,' he said, raising his head to look at me with hooded eyes. In other circumstances, I would have broken my fist on the bearded chin pointing so provocatively towards me.

'Prince Sinter, I thank you for granting me this interview at my request. I have come to apologise.'

His face froze. My statement was clearly the last thing he had expected me to say.

'Go on.'

Though his voice was frosty, I sensed a faint thaw in his manner.

'Your Highness, I chose the wrong time to criticise you and Prince Sigmund after we arrived at Rehschloss early on Christmas morning. You had done our party the courtesy of welcoming us to the safety of the castle, at a time when all should be asleep. I repaid your kindness with an angry outburst and by withdrawing my support.'

He pounced on my omission. 'Hah! You apologise for the time, but not the content!'

I did not rise to the challenge of his reply. When I kept my silence, he tried to provoke me further.

'You know, I arranged to have you killed.'

'Yes, your Highness. I was fortunate that your men at arms went to protect Prince Sigmund from Arnulf's men rather than turn on me.'

'So you guessed!' He snorted a laugh. 'And yet you are still here! Do you still claim you aren't protected by the fairies?'

'With respect, Prince Sinter, my protection was more substantial than fairies that day. Silvio's men warned me. When I fled, they took me under their wing.'

'Oh, yes! I forgot you even consort with outlaws. Is that the end to your apology?'

'It is enough, your Highness. I am here to save Prince Sigmund. Dr Petrus persuaded me that this was a necessary step.'

Sinter roared with laughter. 'Oh, the good doctor! I knew there had to be more than you involved.'

He turned towards the fire to consider the implications of my apology. When he turned back, his face was serious.

'Well, let me cap your story with mine, Gendal. Be seated.'

It was my turn to be nonplussed. I sat where he indicated, on a wooden chair at the other side of the fire, and wished I had taken off my cloak before I had entered his room.

'I too have been told to apologise, to you!' Sinter said, his eyes wide open and his mouth smirking in bemused surprise. 'Rehlein is most cross with me. When he returned here, Sheriff Opecz arrested him as soon as he set foot in the courtyard. This was despite my men reporting Oscar's men for trying to assassinate him en route. My father even had to make special representation to Oscar to grant me permission to see him! They are keeping him prisoner in his own room. He is quite comfortable; but they do restrict who he sees and where he goes.'

'At least he has come to no harm.'

Sinter frowned at the lack of respectful courtesy in my statement, but let it go. He continued:

'We were all surprised that you did not arrive here with Rehlein and his escort, when you had set off with them. Rehlein asked me if I knew what had happened. I told him I had arranged for you to be ambushed and killed on the road. He was so angry, he actually shouted at me! He said, "How can we prove my innocence now, with Gendal gone?" They let me visit him again this morning. I was with him when you turned up. You cannot believe how relieved we were to see you. He told me to apologise at once.'

'Thank you, your Highness. So the well-heeled ruffians in rough cloaks were your men, not someone else's?'

'God, you're so difficult to hoodwink! Yes, they were mine. And they made the mistake of taking on the whole column instead of you and my five men at the rear.'

His lack of remorse astonished me. His admission also made me wonder why Silvio's men had led me to believe the ambush had been Arnulf's doing. Had they truly believed that, or had they simply been using it to get my support in their quest for redress?

Sinter's lightning-fast thoughts changed course yet again. 'So how are you planning to save Rehlein this time, Gendal?'

'I have called a meeting for midday, in the Lesser Hall. I have instructed everyone to attend who was present in the castle on the day of Prince Umbert's death. As the former Imperator's Herald, I will examine all the evidence, without fear or favour.'

'Perfect! You'll be able to turn the findings to our advantage.'

'You have already corrupted my witness once, Prince Sinter. I warn you not to try that again.'

Chapter 23
The Evidence is Heard

The Lesser Hall was crowded with people, from highborn to serfs. The highborn sat on benches and chairs in a semicircle around the edge of the hall. Their knights and squires completed the circle, with the shorter squires standing in front of the household cavalrymen. The ladies sat in the musicians' gallery as they would not normally be called to speak as witnesses. The low-born stood in a group near the door. A semicircle of open floor had been left around the table and benches where Prince Umbert had died, and a fire blazed in the hearth nearby.

A scribe's desk and seat had been placed for me near the far end of the table, to leave the carver chair at its head free for those involved to re-enact their parts in Umbert's death. I took my place at the desk and surveyed the ring of faces. None were unfamiliar, though I would not have been able to name many of them. But one face was missing.

'Where is Prince Sigmund?' I asked.

'He is under arrest, for patricide,' said Opecz.

'Lord Heinrich, bring him here.'

As Henrich left the hall, I raised a silent prayer to God to give me wisdom and skill to handle the hearing ahead. In using my herald's wand, I was about to take on the role of the Imperator and lead the trial of Prince Sigmund by his Lords and Peers, despite being a commoner. The weight of responsibility lay heavily on my shoulders.

'Lord Opecz, pray step forward,' I opened.

Opecz stood up as requested. His confident presence filled the draughty hall, making it feel much smaller. He stood tall, well-muscled, and well dressed for the festival in a belted maroon velvet surcoat over a grey silk shirt and dark wool breeches. His manner was haughty, as if he thought my intervention was unnecessary and beneath him.

'Sheriff Opecz, what were your grounds for arresting Prince Sigmund?' I asked.

'My grounds were the circumstances of Prince Umbert's death, Knight Gendal. Father and son were alone in here, arguing. Prince Umbert cried out. Lord Arnulf ran in to help him. He saw Prince Sigmund forcing his father to drink from a poisoned cup. Arnulf took the cup from his hand, but it was too late: Prince Umbert was already dying. As no-one else was in the room when it happened, it was clearly Prince Sigmund who had committed the crime.'

'And how did you proceed?'

'As sheriff, I sent Prince Sigmund to his room under house arrest and examined the evidence. We discussed trial by combat, or taking the case to the King of Rome for Sigmund to be tried by his peers. Before we had reached a decision, Sigmund absconded.'

'Did you call in a physician to help confirm how Prince Umbert died?'

'Lady Herlinde sent for Brother Matthias from the nearby monastery. But we did not need his advice when we already knew how Prince Umbert had died.'

I looked across the room at the monk who was standing expressionless, his eyes gazing downwards as if he were trying to avoid any contact or interaction with the profane company around him. To save the monk from direct confrontation so early in the proceedings, I moved on to another discrepancy in Opecz's witness.

'Are you still in possession of the cup?'

Opecz's dark eyes shifted briefly, telling me the question had disconcerted him.

'No. It would have been returned to the kitchen.'

'Then how do you know it contained poison?'

'By the effects the drink had on Umbert when Sigmund forced him to swallow it.'

'You did not taste the drink or to check whether it contained anything more than wine?'

'What, and risk killing myself too?'

I produced the goblet Eleanore had given me. She gasped in the gallery above as I placed it on the table. The garnets and cornelians sparkled in the firelight.

'Is this the cup?'

'Possibly. How did you come by it?'

'It was given to me by someone who wanted me to find the truth.

It still contains staining from the last drink Umbert drank: your fine, unadulterated local wine.'

As Opecz blustered a response to cast doubt on the authenticity of the cup, Heinrich entered the hall with Sigmund. No seat had been set out for the accused. Instead, Heinrich guided him to stand between himself and the Castellan.

'That will be all for now, Lord Opecz. Thank you, Lord Heinrich, for your prompt return. Welcome, Prince Sigmund. It appears the only seat free is at this table. Pray, take your seat at the place where you sat when you had your last words with your father.'

Sigmund looked at me in pained horror, but obeyed.

'Knight Klaus, take Prince Umbert's place at the head of the table, beside Prince Sigmund. I want you to show us what happened that day. Lord Arnulf, be ready to replay your part at the appropriate time.'

I placed the goblet on the table beside Sigmund, using the opportunity to whisper some advice in his ear.

'Sigmund, tell the assembly everything you told me on Christmas Eve.'

His head dropped as I sat back down at the scribe's table to continue the examination.

'Prince Sigmund, show our company exactly what happened here at your last meeting with your father, Prince Umbert.'

Sigmund paled, as if I had asked him to do the worst thing he could ever imagine. He summoned that heroic part in himself to obey, and rose to his feet.

'Father and I were arguing. He wanted me to marry, and I refused. He told me I was obliged to marry Lady Eleanore, as he had contracted with the Boesel family for the Crown Prince of Harzland to marry their eldest daughter in a political alliance. I told him I would rather renounce my claim to the throne than marry for political gain. He was furious. He paced the floor, shouting at me. Then he stumbled and the power seemed to leave him. I helped him to the table and sat him in this chair, where Klaus sits now.'

I noted how Sigmund's story had changed yet again, but forbore to comment.

'How did Prince Umbert look?' I asked.

As Sigmund replied, he demonstrated how he had tried to help his father, with Klaus standing in for the dead prince.

'Father sat lopsided. Half his face drooped. He tried to reach for his cup of wine, but there was no strength in his arm. When he spoke, I could not understand him. I thought he was asking me to help him drink. So I picked up the cup and cradled him in my right arm. He needed help to sit up, as he was sliding down off the chair. When I tilted the cup to pour the wine into his mouth, it struck him again. The wine poured down, but he did not swallow. All I saw were his frightened eyes.'

Arnulf sprang across, his long grey surcoat flying.

'I heard Prince Umbert's cry and ran into the hall,' he said. 'I struck the cup out of Prince Sigmund's hand, like so.'

His back-handed blow almost blooded Klaus's nose. The goblet flew through the air and landed on the floor near where Marlena had shown me, about half way down the table.

'Thank you, Lord Arnulf. You may return to your seat. And thank you both for your demonstration, Prince Sigmund and Knight Klaus.'

As Sigmund released Klaus and Arnulf returned to his seat, I turned to look for the monk in the crowd. His white habit made him stand out despite his desire to merge in. When I called him forward, he crossed the floor to place a compassionate hand on Sigmund's shoulder. Then he picked up the goblet and placed it on the table before turning to face me.

'Brother Matthias, as physician, how would you diagnose what had happened to Prince Umbert?' I asked.

'Prince Umbert was struck down in his anger with apoplexy by God's judgement.'

'Could any medicine or potion you know of, have had the same effect?'

'No. Nothing could have acted that quickly. Henbane can cause paralysis, but it would cause many other effects before that. I asked people if they had seen them, but no-one told me they had. Hemlock can also cause similar effects to those described, but they would have affected both sides of the body at the same time, not one after the other as has been testified here.'

'I see: you ruled out poisoning with henbane or hemlock. So, how did Prince Umbert die?'

'He died of the consequences of his sinfulness. His body failed after receiving the two blows from God which struck him down with apoplexy.'

'Did the administration of the cup of wine make any difference to his fate?'

'It only hastened his death. Prince Umbert could not have survived the injuries God had inflicted upon him. When Prince Sigmund gave him the wine he asked for, he saved his father from enduring many days of a cruel and lingering death.'

Sigmund covered his face with his hands and wept. Sinter shifted in his seat as if he wanted to comfort his cousin. I felt relieved to see the arrogant prince still had some vestige of compassion. To give him some time to offer Sigmund support, I called a brief halt to the proceedings.

I went outside for a few moments to reflect on my next steps. The air was crisp and cool, as if a frost would settle that night. In the stillness of the courtyard, I opened my treasured mirror locket and focused on it while praying for guidance.

Before returning to the Lesser Hall, I went to use the garderobe in the Great Hall. As I turned the dogleg in the narrow stone passage to the garderobe itself, a man came from behind to placed a knife against my throat. He grabbed my right hand, pulling my arm up and forward to force my neck onto his blade.

I reacted instinctively, turning my body and head left, away from the blade. Using my full weight, I threw my right shoulder against the wall, crushing the assailant's arm between them. The knife clattered to the floor. Before he could retaliate, I spun round on my right foot, grabbed his shoulders, and threw his body against the wall. His head cracked on the stone. He slithered to the floor, stunned. I picked up the knife and left him lying there.

On my way back to the Lesser Hall, I met the Castellan heading in the same direction, and handed him the knife I had confiscated.

'I left the owner in the garderobe. He made the mistake of trying to ambush me. Pick him up and sort him out, will you?' I said.

The Castellan nodded with a look of astonishment and watched me walk off back into the Lesser Hall.

The crowded hall fell silent when I entered. I took my place at the scribe's desk, with much more confidence in what I was doing. The incident had been an effective, if unnerving, answer to my prayer for guidance.

Sigmund had been given a seat between his brother Oscar and his cousin Sinter during my short absence. I felt encouraged to see the repair in family relationships already taking place due to my intervention.

'Your Royal Highness, Prince Volkmar, would you be willing to speak as a witness in this hearing?' I asked.

Volkmar responded with a regal nod of condescension. A smile flickered on his lips as he calculated the reasoning behind my tactics. He elected to answer my questions from the comfort of his well-cushioned chair.

'Your Highness, what was your reaction when you learned that Prince Sigmund had been arrested for murdering his father?'

Volkmar's smile became crooked with irascible pleasure at being given the floor so openly.

'It was a travesty of justice!' he cried. 'Sigmund never wanted the responsibility of the crown. His head was stuffed full of dreams of being a hero. He gained nothing by his father's death, and only lost. But others had a lot to gain by finding him guilty.'

'Your Highness, can you see those other people in this gathering today?'

'I can.' His fierce gaze shifted down the line of seated nobles to his right, which included Oscar, Opecz, Arnulf, Heinrich and Klaus, and beyond them the Castellan and the Chamberlain.

'Your Highness, did you express your concerns at the time?'

'Of course I did! I put a stop to the suggestion of trial by combat, as we all knew Oscar had no chance of beating Sigmund. I didn't want Lady Herlinde to lose her two sons as well as her husband. Then when they talked of taking Sigmund to be tried by his peers, I put a stop to that too. Who knows who would have survived a long journey like that to petition the court of Louis, our self-styled King of Rome! So I arranged for Sigmund's escape. Once he had left Harzland, I returned home to Schwarzenberg with my son, Prince Sinter.'

'When did you next hear of Prince Sigmund, your highness?'

'I received a letter from Sigmund, late summer, asking for some help with an uprising in Danuvia. The cause was such a folly, I knew at once he was seeking an honourable death to assuage his guilt. So I sent Sinter off with a cohort of our troops to support him. My son persuaded Sigmund to abandon such folly and return to the safety of Schwarzenberg. And that is all I am prepared to say. Address the rest of your questions to Sinter!'

'Thank you, your Highness, for indulging me for so long.'

I bowed to him and turned my attention to his son as instructed.

'Prince Sinter, if I may, pray tell us how you brought Prince Sigmund out of danger at the battle of Dernfels, to the safety of your ancestral home.'

Sinter rested his head on his left hand and regarded me with a warning look before he answered me. With his flowing black hair and trimmed beard, and his unblinking eyes, he looked like a crow in human form.

'I laid a false trail. My men dressed two casualties in our surcoats and helmets shortly after we had departed the field. You saw the bodies on the field and assumed what I had intended. And like the good messenger you are, you took the news of our deaths to our nearest and dearest as soon as you were able.'

Though he was deliberately trying to provoke me, I was more impressed by his attempt to shoulder all the blame for the plot. He was making sure his cousin's reputation became as pure as circumstances would allow.

'Was that all you planned for me to do, your Highness?'

He barked a short laugh. 'Of course not. I knew that when you turned up and told Oscar his brother was dead, you would realise the wrong son had been given the crown. I knew you would not let that lie: you are so committed to justice, you had to find out why it had happened. And that is why we are all here today!'

He smirked at us all, puppets in the show he had created.

'And now, you are going to tell us what really happened, aren't you, Ministerialis,' he instructed.

'I will, your Highness, but not just yet,' I said.

The flash of fire in the look he sent me for resisting him, was not lost on those present.

Undaunted, I explained, 'First, I need to demonstrate how I arrived at my conclusions. For that, we must await the arrival of the people from Rehschloss.'

Chapter 24
The Unmasking

The hearing restarted in the late afternoon. The Lesser Hall was crowded again. Though many of the servants had returned to their routine tasks, others had replaced them, curious to see how the hearing would end.

'Page Goswin, come forward,' I ordered.

The young lad obeyed, trembling. Dr Petrus walked out with him and stood by him in support. Goswin's gaze strayed across the gathering of nobles staring at him. His eyes widened in terror. Petrus whispered in his ear, encouraging him to look at my face and that alone.

'Goswin, do you remember the day after you first met me?' I asked, my tone gentle and encouraging.

He nodded.

'Can you tell me what happened that day?'

I could not hear his reply. Petrus encouraged him to repeat what he had said more loudly.

'I brought you your breakfast. Then I made ready your horse, Finstar. I watched what the other pages and squires were doing to ready their knights for training, and I did the same.'

'When did you bring Finstar to me?'

'It was after noon. You were training with the household cavalry. The sparring had finished. Your next exercise was riding with the lance along the list wall. The other knights soon finished catching all the rings, but you didn't. I don't think you had done it before. But you kept trying, and I was proud of how you never gave up. Then I realised why Lord Heinrich had made me your page, not one of the other pages, for you can't have been noble-born either, to have had no learning with the lance.'

His observation drew a gentle laugh from the crowd, which made him blush.

'Well thought, Goswin: ignore the other people,' I said. 'What happened next?'

'You were the last on the tilting field. Only I stayed with you, putting the rings back up for you to hook on the lance again. All the other knights were practising with the quintains. As you made another pass for the rings, a grey lancer came riding at you up the other side of the tilt wall, aiming for your body. I shouted to warn you. You pulled Finstar away. He stumbled and you fell. I ran to fetch you a sword and buckler. Then I saw the grey lancer trying to ride you down. I thought you were done for when you dropped to the ground. But you rolled out of the way as the lancer passed. Then you got up and ran towards me, and the lancer rode off.'

'Did you recognise the grey lancer?'

'No. But I knew the horse. It was a bay gelding with a white blaze and two white socks. I found him in the courtyard when I went to stable Finstar. So I stabled them both in the cavalry stables. By next morning he had gone.'

I realised I had overlooked something as simple as identifying the horse to trace the rider. When I asked my next question, I hoped Goswin had been mindful enough to do that for me.

'Have you seen the horse since?'

'Yes, and I have seen him before. He's the horse Prince Oscar rides.'

A murmur of speculation rose up from the crowd. I thanked Goswin and instructed him to return with Dr Petrus to the crowd. Then I called Klaus forward. The young man obeyed, looking disconcerted to see my formal bearing towards him after our previous camaraderie of the road.

'Knight Klaus, would you describe what happened the day after the incident in the training field which Page Goswin has just described?'

'Of course, Knight Gendal. That was the day you left Harzberg early to ride to Schwarzenberg with the news of Prince Sinter's death. Lady Herlinde sent me to join you on the road as she feared for your safety. When I caught up with you, we stopped to rest the horses at a wayside inn. I had ridden my horse hard to catch up with you. That vexed you because you wanted to reach Kreuzbruke that night.'

'Go on.'

'We set off early afternoon and kept a gentle pace. Our road took us through the thickest part of the forest. We suddenly heard some shouting from behind. Four horsemen attacked us. Two lancers went for you. Two with axes attacked me. I may have bettered you at lancing the quoits, but you certainly bettered me in real combat.'

'Even so, your being there saved my life. Pray, tell everyone present why you had asked Lady Herlinde permission to be excused from your training so that you could ride after me?'

'I had overheard at dinner the evening before, a man saying they were going to clip an eagle's wings. As you are the only one at dinner wearing an eagle as your badge, I knew it was a threat against you.'

'And is that person in this hall today?' I asked, letting yet another discrepancy pass for the moment.

Klaus' eyes flicked briefly to the same place that Prince Volkmar's eyes had done. He said, 'Yes. And the person he said it to is here too.'

Whispers of speculation buzzed among the crowd. The people expected me to instruct Klaus to point out who it was, but I did not want to spring my trap too soon.

I dismissed Klaus from giving testimony and waited for him to return to his place with the household cavalry before I spoke again. The air was tense with speculation. I looked around at all the faces and wished my duty had fallen to someone else.

'Your Royal Highnesses, my Lords and Ladies, and all others present here today, as Knight Ministerialis and Herald, I shall now reveal my findings without fear or favour. Pray be quiet unless I ask you to speak.'

The room fell silent. The only sound came from the logs crackling in the fire.

'On the First of May this year, Prince Umbert argued with his son Prince Sigmund in this hall, at this table. Prince Umbert was not a well man. Despite his ruddy complexion, his body was failing after years of hard living. He wanted to ensure his family line continued beyond his sons. To that end, he arranged a marriage pact with the Boesel family for his son, the crown prince, to marry Lady Eleanore. Prince Sigmund refused outright, He would not even consider marrying Eleanore and leaving her to languish alone in Rehschloss while he went off adventuring, as Prince Umbert suggested to him. To Prince Umbert, breaking that contract would have caused him the most serious loss of face – it was the worst thing he could countenance. He was furious with his son and told him so in no uncertain terms.

'As he did so, apoplexy struck him down. Prince Sigmund saw the change in his father and tried to help him, supporting him at the table, and giving him a drink of wine when he asked. Despite refusing his father over the marriage pact, he acted only as the dutiful son in his need.'

I sipped some water to give space for my audience to appreciate the point I had made.

'It was at that point Lord Arnulf ran in from the courtyard, having heard Prince Umbert's cry. Lord Arnulf assessed the situation to be an attack on his benefactor and acted with commendable decisiveness, dashing the goblet from Prince Sigmund's hand with such force that it dented the rim when it hit the flagstone floor. The wine it held splashed across the table.'

Arnulf nodded with a satisfied smile to hear my opinion of his reaction.

'When Lord Opecz and others ran in from the courtyard, Lord Arnulf told them all he had just stopped Prince Sigmund from poisoning his father, an understandable conclusion to make from what he had seen. Lord Opecz, as Sheriff, arrested Prince Sigmund and had him confined to his room. When Lord Opecz investigated, he came to the same conclusion as Lord Arnulf, that Prince Umbert had been murdered by his son.'

The two Lords nodded vigorously.

'What I do not understand is, why did Lord Opecz not take into account what Brother Matthias said after Lady Herlinde had asked the monk for his expert opinion? Instead of finding this a tragic accident, the Sheriff called for trial by combat, risking the deaths of the two sons in addition to their father. When Prince Volkmar stopped this, they then called for trial by Prince Sigmund's peers, which would have involved half the court undertaking a perilous journey to Upper Bavaria. Lord Opecz, can you explain yourself here?'

'I live in the real world, not shut off from reality in a cloister,' Opecz replied with that arrogant insouciance I had often seen in members of his class. 'Prince Umbert cried out. We entered to find Sigmund pouring poisoned wine down his throat. We stopped him. Despite that, our illustrious Prince Umbert died. Of course, Sigmund poisoned him. We just had to prove it in law.'

I thanked him with a certain reserve and continued my assessment.

'Our illustrious guests from the House of Schwarzenberg, Prince Volkmar and Prince Sinter, told us how they stepped in to save Prince Sigmund from injustice by helping him to escape. This is where I come to the second matter I do not understand. Prince Sigmund had not actually been found guilty of anything. Yet there seemed to be undue haste in declaring Prince Oscar the new crown prince, enthroning him, and solemnising his marriage to Lady Eleanore, who is now already full with child following that union. Prince Oscar, are you able to explain this?'

Oscar's head was down and his shoulders were slumped. He straightened himself in his chair to answer me. His voice was so subdued, I could barely hear him.

'I was advised that my brother's disappearance proved his guilt. Our father's death had left a political void which some of our more rapacious neighbours would seek to fill if we did not name his successor at once. It was politically expedient for me to be crowned in Prince Umbert's stead with all speed and to wed my beloved Eleanore.'

'Who were your advisors?'

'My uncle Lord Heinrich, our Sheriff Lord Opecz, and Lord Arnulf.'

I would have liked to ask Herlinde what she had thought of such political expediency, but refrained. It would not have been appropriate to oblige her to give evidence in such a gathering, and I could not trust Oscar to answer truthfully on her behalf. I thanked Oscar and continued my assessment.

'After some months, I came across Prince Sigmund in Strasbourg and persuaded him to travel with me. We became caught up in the Rabenwald rebellion against the Duke of Danuvia. Prince Sigmund appealed to his cousin and his great uncle for help. Yet again, Prince Sinter came to his assistance and laid a false trail, making it appear as if he and Prince Sigmund had both died in battle, when in fact they had ridden back to the safety of Schwarzenberg Castle. There they hid and waited for me to bring their families the news of their deaths.'

Sinter's glower warned me to take great care. I gave a wry laugh.

'Unfortunately, I was delayed by various mishaps. When I finally did arrive at Harzberg to break the bad news, I was surprised to find it received with a sense of relief rather than mourning. Prince Oscar's reminiscences about his elder brother Sigmund made me wonder why the younger prince had been crowned in preference to the older. I began to ask questions. Then more mishaps occurred: as you have heard, the unknown lancer at the lists, and the ambush on the way to Schwarzenberg, among others. These only made me more determined to uncover the truth. I must thank all of you for your patience in answering my questions. Each clue has built into the picture I have now.'

I drank to slake my dry mouth. It was time to conclude in what was likely to turn into a fiery confrontation.

'The final question I had to answer was, who would benefit most from this? I saw Lord Heinrich controlling Prince Oscar's affairs and keeping his sister Lady Herlinde from outside contact, and naturally suspected him. When I arrived with the message of Prince Sigmund's death, Lord Heinrich obstructed me at every turn and insulted me with his choice of page. Did this reflect his guilt? Had he used his influence over Oscar to manoeuvre the younger prince into the throne after Prince Umbert's death for his own ends? Had he hastened the coronation and the wedding to ensure that after Prince Sigmund decamped, he no longer had a claim to the throne? But no: I saw that Lord Heinrich had simply wanted to protect Prince Oscar and Lady Herlinde: to save them from the impact of the bad news I had brought and the sad memories my presence would bestir.'

Heinrich sank back in his chair with a sigh of relief. In the gallery above, Lady Herlinde stifled a sob of relief. I continued.

'What I also saw was the hold two other people had over Lord Heinrich, and through him, over Prince Oscar. These influential people had taken care not to come to my notice, but their names came up as soon as I started asking questions about Prince Umbert's death. Lord Arnulf had accused Prince Sigmund of patricide, and Lord Opecz had arrested him, ignoring the testimony of Brother Matthias. These two Lords had arrived at this court only six years ago. Prince Umbert had made Lord Opecz sheriff just one year ago, after the former sheriff became too frail to continue this exacting role. But why did they come here, and where had they come from? Dr Petrus, come forward.'

Petrus emerged from the crowd, bringing a black folder with him, which he placed carefully on the table at my instruction.

'Dr Petrus, tell us what you have dedicated your life to since the children you taught have grown too old for your classroom.'

'Knight Gendal, I am making a study of the heraldic crests found in the different states of the Holy Roman Empire.'

'Would you like to show everyone present one of the heraldic badges you showed me?'

'Certainly, Knight Gendal.'

He opened the black folder and took out the page showing Opecz's crest of two azure wavy lines on an argent field.

'This is Lord Opecz's family crest. His family held a fief bestowed by the Duke of Romfeld.'

'Do you have another you can show us?'

'I have many. Here is the family crest of Lord Arnulf Althaus. His family also held a fief bestowed by the Duke of Romfeld.'

He held up a page showing two crossed falchions in gold on a vert field.

'Thank you, Dr Petrus. Do you know why Lord Arnulf and Lord Opecz now have positions of authority here, instead of ruling their own fiefs under the Duke of Romfeld's recognisance?'

'They lost their fiefs about six years ago, when the Duke of Romfeld evicted them for mismanagement and cruelty.'

'Lies, all lies!' Arnulf shouted.

'These are just rumours,' Opecz protested.

'Lords, I instructed you to be quiet unless I ask you to speak. If you cannot, I will have you removed from this hall so that I can complete this hearing without interruption.'

They slumped back in their seats with sullen faces, knowing it was better to stay and hear my findings than to be forcibly removed and miss the rest. I noticed Opecz giving a veiled hand signal to someone in the crowd near the door. Three people left the hall.

'Thank you, Dr Petrus. Please stand down,' I said. After he had returned to the crowd, I continued my review of the evidence.

'Our two Lords, Arnulf and Opecz, arrived about the time Prince Umbert was feeling the consequences of his hard life. They ingratiated themselves and quickly rose to prominence in the court here at Harzberg. They gave invaluable service to the ailing Prince, with their previous experience of running their fiefs. When the old sheriff became too infirm to carry out his duties, Umbert promoted Opecz to take his place. Then they waited for their opportunity.'

Arnulf and Opecz shifted in their seats and regarded me with wary eyes. Their hands moved to their hips.

I continued, 'When Umbert died in Sigmund's arms, they turned the tragedy to their advantage, seeing an opportunity to win not only a comfortable home for life, but this whole principality. They accused Sigmund of murdering Umbert and called for trial by combat in the hope of seeing both princes killed. That would have left the land without a rightful heir, and opened the way for them to seize the crown themselves. But Prince Volkmar recognised the dangers and intervened. They then called for trial by the Princes' peers, which Prince Volkmar again blocked, realising the very real dangers the brothers could face during the journey involved.

'Sigmund absconded, thwarting their plans. When I arrived with the news of his death and started asking questions, they tried to stop me. It was you, Lord Arnulf, who attacked me at the list, riding Prince Oscar's horse to cast the blame on him!'

'Enough!' Arnulf roared.

He leapt up, grasped Oscar's neck in an armlock and dragged

him to his feet, his dagger pressed against his ribs. Opecz bounded from his seat to pull Volkmar up by his fur collar. He placed his dagger across his neck. Thirty members of the household cavalry came out of the crowd in their support, a third of all Oscar's mounted men at arms.

Arnulf and Opecz pulled their victims halfway across the hall and paused with their backs against each other.

'Don't try to stop us, or your two fine princes will die!' Arnulf threatened.

Opecz growled and mimed slitting Volkmar's throat.

They dragged their victims out of the hall into the courtyard. The thirty cavalrymen moved across to protect their rear and followed them out. Sinter, Sigmund and I leapt from our seats to stop the upstarts, but were helpless to save their hostages. The heavy hall doors slammed shut behind the traitors, and they were gone.

Chapter 25
The Traitors Flee

Sinter and Sigmund ran across the Lesser Hall to open the doors into the courtyard. I chased after them. We found the heavy oak doors had been blocked by some obstruction. They held fast, even when the three of us threw ourselves against them at the same time. We tried the door to the main staircase and found that blocked too.

Herlinde's deep, melodic voice called out to us across the hall.

'Sigmund! Sinter! This way.'

She was standing by a brocade curtain which she had raised to reveal the ladies' entrance to the hall. We dashed through the open doorway and up the narrow stone staircase to the Royal Apartments above. From there, we ran down the main staircase to the Great Hall and out into the courtyard.

Opecz and Arnulf were riding out with their followers through the main gate as we emerged, some thirty-five men or more. On the cobbles before us lay Oscar and Volkmar. Sigmund and Sinter ran to help them.

I turned back to free the doors to the Lesser Hall. The traitors had secured them by slotting a bar through the outer handles to wedge them shut. I pulled out the bar and pushed the doors back. A crowd of people streamed out into the courtyard. Their indignant voices deafened me as they complained about their treatment to each other. I ignored them and went back to see if the princes needed my help.

Oscar lay unconscious on the cobbles, blood streaming from his nose after being knocked out by a blow from Arnulf. Volkmar was sitting on the ground where Opecz had thrown him, calling out a stream of indignant curses as he waved his fist after his long gone assailant.

Sinter gathered up his frail father in his arms with great tenderness and carried him back inside the Lesser Hall. He sat him by the fire to warm him and found cushions to make his seat more comfortable. The fury in the young prince's eyes chilled my blood.

Brother Matthias was concerned that Oscar was still unconscious and checked his injuries. He helped Sigmund lift Oscar's heavy body off the cobbles and carry him back inside the hall. They laid him on the table where Umbert had died. Brother Matthias sent a message to the kitchen for supplies to treat Oscar's wounds and asked Herlinde for smelling salts to bring him round.

As the princes did not need me, I ran to the gatehouse to ask the sentry which way the horsemen had gone. He stood leaning back against the wall, his face pale and streaked with blood pouring from a deep gash across his cheek.

'What's happened?' I demanded.

'I tried to stop them. Sheriff Opecz slashed me,' he gasped, wincing with pain.

'Which way did they go?'

The effort of pointing down the hill towards the river made his legs give way. I lifted him up and put his arm round my shoulder to take him to be treated in the Lesser Hall. As we crossed the courtyard, Klaus came over to us.

'Prince Volkmar is unharmed, if a little peppery, and Prince Oscar has come round,' he reported. 'What's happened here?'

'Opecz returning to his old, savage ways,' I said. 'We're off to find Brother Matthias. Can you close the gates? We need to stop them coming back tonight for another go.'

'Yes, sir! I'll get some men to drop the portcullis and bar the main gate.'

'Don't forget the postern gate in the herb garden. Make sure that is locked and barred too.'

Klaus hurried off to do my bidding. I helped the sentry cross the courtyard to the Lesser Hall. The hall now felt like a haven of quiet after the hubbub of the crowd outside; but not for long. As soon as I had handed the sentry over to the care of Brother Matthias, Sinter rose from supporting his father to turn on me.

'Why did you not tell me they were rogues? I would have dealt with them before they showed their true colours. Your mistakes allowed them to seize my father! It is your fault they put his life at risk!'

'My reason was the same as yours, Prince Sinter, when you

didn't tell me your plans,' I answered coldly. 'I was not sure of their guilt until they felt provoked to act. I didn't want the slightest hint to warn them.'

Volkmar was shivering by the fire from the after-effects of shock. His caring wife, Ilse, stood with him, noble in her favourite red brocade and green velvet gown. Some of the vigour had gone from her stance. She draped his fur cloak back around his trembling shoulders and held his right hand. I crouched down before him.

'Forgive me, your Highness, for placing you in such danger.'

He cackled. 'It drew the pus out of the wound, though. You did well, Messenger. The family honour of Hirschmann and Schwarzenberg is repaired. That's an end to this sorry episode.'

'Alas, your Highness, knowing their reputation, I think not.'

And sadly, I was right.

Chapter 26
Reprisals

Harzberg held a subdued observance of the Feast of Sylvester. Though Oscar presided over the castle's traditional banquet and stayed at the gathering the whole evening until we had seen in the New Year, it was not the usual riotous party. The musicians played in the gallery but the mummers did not perform in the hall.

We began Anno Domine 1320 with a belated start to New Year's Day. The kitchen laid out a late morning meal in the Lesser Hall for Oscar's guests. As the hall had been out of regular use since Prince Umbert's death, it was encouraging to see how the hearing the day before had rehabilitated that part of the castle in addition to

Sigmund's reputation.

A few guests joined Oscar for the communal meal, the rest choosing to eat in their chambers. Most of the guests were entering the hall as I left. Oscar was enjoying the role of the genial host again despite his previous day's adventures. His face was pale but otherwise he looked well. He appreciated being among people he knew he could trust. Volkmar looked none the worse for his abduction. He and Ilse had breakfast with the Moltké family, and spent far more time talking to them than eating.

The courtyard was busy with horsemen when I came outside. Sinter's fifty cavalrymen had joined the household cavalry still loyal to Oscar, swelling their number. Goswin was leading Finstar out for me to ride out with them, when we heard the sound of dragging wood, the noise made when the gatekeeper raised the outer portcullis. We watched the main gate open.

Steward Dietl cantered into the courtyard, his chestnut mare sweating after a hard ride from Rehschloss

'Rehschloss is overrun!' he gasped. 'Lord Opecz and Lord Arnulf have taken it over!'

I helped Dietl dismount and gave Goswin the reins of both his horse and mine to take care of them back. When Klaus saw the condition of the mare, he ran across to join Dietl and me as we crossed the courtyard to the Great Hall.

'What has happened, Gendal? Is there anything I can do?'

'Plenty, Klaus,' I said. 'The reprisals have begun. Call the Princes out from breakfast and ask them to go to the Great Hall. But be discreet about it.'

'Of course,' he said with a wry smile. He walked away to the Lesser Hall to carry out my instruction.

I took Dietl into the Great Hall and persuaded him to sit down on one of the benches. A servant came to light a fire from the hot ashes in the massive stone fireplace. Oscar, Sigmund and Sinter quickly joined us, and Heinrich arrived soon after them. Dietl showed his deference to his lords by trying to get back to his feet again. He was so unsteady, Sigmund insisted he sat back down. Oscar and Sinter stood back to let Sigmund handle the steward as the man worked for him.

Sigmund sat beside Dietl to encourage him.

'What has happened?' he asked.

'Your Highness, Lord Opecz and Lord Arnulf have taken over Rehschloss! Their men are causing havoc! They've claimed the fief as their own.'

'Is there no end to their wilfulness? Do they still try to usurp you, Prince Oscar?' Sinter said.

'What actually happened, Dietl?' Sigmund asked. His calm manner helped Dietl become calmer, too.

'Lord Opecz and Lord Arnulf arrived yesterday, mid-evening, with a force of men. They claimed you sent them, Prince Oscar, so we had no cause to doubt them. We made them welcome, with food and lodging. Then they turned on us.'

'You did right to welcome them, Dietl,' Sigmund said; 'You weren't to know what happened here yesterday. How did they abuse your hospitality?'

'They drank their fill over dinner. Then Lord Arnulf announced Rehschloss and its lands were now his and Lord Opecz's. Their men all cheered and went to claim their possession. They forced themselves on our women, and killed any who refused them.'

He broke down and sobbed. I put my hand on his shoulder to console him.

'How did you get away?' I asked to distract him from the horror and betrayal he was reliving.

'I told the gateman this morning I had to check on one of the farms. He let me out and shut the gate behind me. They hit him when he didn't open it fast enough again. They chased after me, but I lost them down the poachers' runs.'

He pushed his matted hair off his face, leaving a streak of blood across the back of his hand

'You're injured, Dietl!' I said. I looked up at the others. 'Is Brother Matthias still here?'

'Yes,' said Heinrich; 'He's been enjoying his enforced break away from the cloister. I'll fetch him.'

As Heinrich left the hall, Dietl cried out, 'The abbey! The abbey! You must warn Father Abbot! They're going to sack the monastery in revenge.'

'That will be to avenge Brother Matthias' testimony,' said Sinter to his cousins. He turned to me. 'Gendal, instruct our forces to exercise only in the castle grounds this morning. Send messengers to the gatekeepers to shut the city gates. Then fetch the Castellan and the Chamberlain here.'

Sinter's quick-witted command of the situation impressed me. I looked at Oscar for permission to do his cousin's bidding. When he nodded, I hurried out to obey.

The Castellan took no finding: he was organising the mounted cavalry in the courtyard. I gave him Sinter's orders and heard him send out three of the knights to ride to the city gates as I went off in search of the Chamberlain. After checking the royal apartments, I found the Chamberlain in the kitchens discussing menus with the cooks. He dropped what he was doing and followed me back to the Great Hall.

The three cousins were planning tactics with the Castellan when we joined them. A short distance away from them and closer to the fire, Brother Matthias was bandaging the cut in Dietl's scalp.

'Castellan, are you able to organise the city force, as well as the men at arms?' Sinter asked.

'Yes, your Highness. Our townsmen are well-trained. We will send orders to their captains to ready themselves.'

'Chamberlain, how prepared is the castle and the city for a siege?' Sinter asked.

'We can withstand a reasonably long siege, your Highness,' the Chamberlain replied: 'We had a good harvest. Our stores can support us for at least three months, and our water supplies are secure.'

Sinter questioned the Chamberlain and Castella further in a way that would help guide Oscar through the crisis without usurping his authority. After he had gleaned all the information Oscar would need, he handed the decision-making back to his younger cousin with a question where he had already provided the answers.

'Can we then agree on our course of action, Oscar?'

'Indeed,' Oscar said: 'We return Brother Matthias to the monastery with an escort of twenty horsemen to warn Father Abbot, as soon as the Brother has finished here. Ten men will stay to defend the House of God, and the other ten will return here. We will offer an escort to those of our guests who choose to leave our hospitality early. Lord Heinrich, you will organise that. The escorts will come from our own horsemen. Our Castellan will prepare our forces for action against the usurpers, and our Chamberlain will prepare our castle and city for siege.'

Lord Heinrich, the Castellan and the Chamberlain bowed and left the hall to carry out their orders.

'What would you have me do, Prince Oscar?' I asked.

'You claimed a Herald's right of non-involvement. I can only ask you to observe.'

'No herald's wand constrains my hand now, your Highness, unless you want me to parley terms with Lord Arnulf and Lord Opecz.'

'Never!' said Sinter with such venom I shuddered in the face of his hatred.

'What do you think you should do, Gendal?' asked Sigmund.

A commotion outside stopped us. Klaus brought in a distraught cottager wearing a cloak and shoes fashioned from sackcloth, and a torn and muddy dress.

'They've torched our hamlet! They murdered our father and took away our Anna,' she cried. She threw herself at Oscar's feet. 'I beg of you, please help us!'

Her distress cut me to the core. The villainy of the traitors infuriated me. I wanted to throw away all constraint and go out at once to stop them. But this situation demanded a cool head, rational thinking and sound preparation. I reined in my emotions and turned my thoughts to strategy instead.

'Let me go and scout out our foe for you, Prince Oscar,' I offered: 'To hide my tracks, I can ride for the monastery with Brother Matthias, and leave his escort when it's safe to do so.'

'That is sound,' Sinter said.

'And could be very dangerous,' Sigmund warned.

Oscar took their comments as guidance and nodded in agreement. 'Thank you for your brave offer, Knight Gendal. You have our leave to go and do as you suggest.'

'Yes, do what must be done, Cara Gendal,' Sigmund said, with cryptic emphasis.

His hint made me suspect that the escort for Brother Matthias was a deliberate attempt to draw attention to the journey, as if their plan was to use the monk as bait. It was the sort of scheme Sinter would have hatched: wily and manipulative.

'I will go with you, Gendal,' Klaus offered.

I shuddered at the thought of such a novice accompanying me on so perilous a quest.

'Thank you, Klaus, but no. This I must do on my own.'

Chapter 27
Preparations

I rode out with twenty of Harzland's finest young knights, escorting Brother Matthias to the monastery. The white-robed monk sat astride the plodding grey donkey which had brought him to the castle the day before. Beside me rode Knight Klaus, charged by Oscar to act as messenger for the monastery and myself, despite my recommendation that he should stay to defend Harzberg.

Only four of Oscar's guests had asked to be escorted home. Sinter insisted that his father and mother, Prince Volkmar and Lady Ilse, stayed in the safety of the castle. The Moltkés, with their daughters Marlena and Aglé, chose to do so too. They knew any travellers would be vulnerable to attack by the renegades on the winter roads. Sinter also believed the traitors would specifically target Volkmar for being the original architect of their downfall. He wanted to keep his parents safely in his care.

Ribbons of ethereal mist garlanded the trees as our paired column of twenty cavalrymen escorted Brother Matthias along the mile of road to the monastery. Klaus and I rode either side of the plodding donkey, giving me an opportunity to talk with the monk.

'Did you fully consider hemlock, Brother? I have heard strange reports about all it can do when taken,' I said.

He gave an indulgent smile. 'As I said yesterday, hemlock would not have paralysed one side of the body alone.'

'We had only his testimony. Could someone have given him the words to say?'

'Only God can look in to the hearts of men. It is well as it is done.'

'But this has brought the wrath of evil men down on your sacred house. You could forfeit all if your judgement was untrue.'

'My judgement was not false. Therefore God will defend our sacred house. These evil men will die in any undertaking they try against us.'

'Even when Prince Sinter is deliberately setting you house up as a target, by making such a performance out of returning you there?'

'God's will shall prevail against the evil of the day.'

'Then I pray God will defend us too.'

Shortly before the column reached the monastery, I slipped away through the trees to join the track Sigmund had taken us down on Christmas Eve. From the shelter of the forest, I watched the column of cavalrymen turn off the road and ride through the open monastery gates to deliver their charge. Klaus went in with them to warn the Abbot and the Prior of the threat against the monastery.

I turned back to my task. My path through the forest was much easier to follow in daylight without the covering of snow. The trees bore witness to Sigmund's claim that the track was regularly maintained. I thought of Dr Petrus riding this way to discuss matters with the monks and buy his precious inks and paper from them; and Sigmund's use of it in the past for his youthful assignations.

Finstar kept a reasonable pace and made good time. It was still mid-afternoon when we arrived at the last bend, curling round out of the trees onto the open hillside. The valley of fields and farmsteads spread out below us, with Rehschloss standing proudly on the far side. At first glance, all looked well.

I dismounted to let Finstar rest while I studied the landscape. The farmland below was good arable ground. Among the winter fields, plumes of smoke rose from houses and farmyards, plumes too thick to be just the smoke from a hearth. On the rocky outcrop above the fields stood the old rubble and ashlar castle, its heavy gates shut and its portcullis down. The pennants on the towers had changed. They now carried the blue on white and gold on green colours of Opecz and Arnulf, not the red and white pennants of Oscar and Sigmund. A column of thick smoke poured heavenward from inside the castle. I wondered what sort of vandalism had caused the fire. Were they burning the books? Or the half-timbered buildings?

Hands grabbed me from behind: one across my mouth, the other round my waist; pulling me back into the underbrush between the trees. When I struggled, their grip tightened, but they did not take my dagger from my belt. I relaxed, trusting my captors were allies.

They dragged me deeper into the trees. The man carrying me was a big and powerful unwashed brigand in furs who held me as easily as if I were a sheep. His smaller fur-clad companion followed with Finstar. After some distance, they released me and put their fingers to their lips in a warning to be quiet.

Face to face, I recognised them as two of Silvio's wild men of the woods: big Jaan and wily Jack. We had met when I had stayed at their camp between Christmas and the Feast of Sylvester.

'You almost rode straight into their patrol!' hissed Jaan.

'Whose? Opecz and Arnulf?' I whispered in reply.

He nodded. 'Whatever you did, boy, were they mad when they

talked their way into the castle last night.'

'I honoured my pledge to your band of men. I held a formal inquest and challenged the two lords about their past. They decamped, so proving their guilt.'

'They're taking their revenge on the villeins and the serfs.'

'I'm here to try and stop them. How many men have they mustered in their support?'

'Besides their liveried horsemen? They've picked up at least twenty rogues: professional soldiers living rough and looking for a war to join.'

'I need to lure them all away from here.'

He shook his head. 'They're having too much fun. They'll kill you.'

'I want them to find out Brother Matthias has gone back to his monastery.'

A big grin spread across Jaan's broad face. 'Oh, I'm sure Jack here can do that for you!'

His companion nodded, also grinning.

'But how?'

'We'll betray you to them.'

My heart pounded. The problem dealing with outlaws is that they can never be trusted. 'How?' I asked again.

'Act like you hadn't met us. Ride round that bend like you nearly did before. When you see the sentries, cry out in surprise. Then canter back the way you came. We'll throw ourselves on the ground like we tried to stop you. When they pick us up, we'll spin the yarn.'

'What about your own safety? They're as likely to kill you too as listen to you.'

'We'll ask to join them,' said Jack. 'Some of the rogues they've taken on, we'll have no bother.'

'But then you'll be fighting against us, against your own brothers and sisters in the woods.'

'Once we know enough, we'll be gone,' said Jaan: 'You don't think we were here by chance, do you?'

I considered their plan with great trepidation, as it was my life they would be putting on the line. Only Brother Matthias' confidence emboldened me to trust that God's will would prevail against the evil of the day. After a brief prayer for God's protection, I agreed, 'All right. Let's do it.'

They led me back through the trees to the bend in the track where they had first caught me. I mounted Finstar and rode round the curve onto the open hillside. As the outlaws had warned, only fifty yards away stood two sentries wearing the crossed falchion device of Lord Arnulf.

'Whoa!' I cried to draw their attention, shouting as if Finstar had tried to buck me from my saddle. I turned him to face the way I had come and galloped off back into the woods.

As I rode out of the bend, the two brigands sprinted along the path ahead of me, yelling at me to stop. When I passed them, they threw themselves to the ground as if I had ridden over them. The sentries soon caught up with them.

'The bastard!' shouted big Jaan, shaking his fist at my receding back; 'That's all the thanks we get, for helping get Brother Matthias home!'

'Who's that?' demanded the sentries.

'Oh, some knight called Gendal,' said Jack.

By that time, I was some distance away down the road. Once out of sight, I took a narrow turning off the track and up through the wooded hillside to lose them. The track meandered through the trees, ascending gently, and eventually curved round the other side of the hill. It brought me to an open view of the river and the main road running along its south bank.

It was late afternoon, with dusk darkening the skies in the east. Dotted across the landscape were the cottages and farmsteads of the people who worked the land and helped make the wealth of the principality. Smoke billowed from several buildings, not the comforting thin curls of cottage fires, but the thick black columns of burning houses and barns. The wanton destruction sickened me. I abhorred these powerful men who had laid waste the living of so many humble people, purely for spite and revenge.

Guilt engulfed me for unleashing so much terror on such undeserving and unprepared innocents. Although I had been given several warnings about the two renegade lords, I had not expected the scale of the vengeance they would wreak upon the land after being unmasked. Then reason stepped in, reminding me that the guilt lay firmly on the shoulders of the men who had committed such barbarous acts, not on mine for exposing them.

I turned Finstar to ride on along the track. Soon our way took us down the hillside, heading away from the burning cottages and towards Harzberg.

The city gates were shut when I arrived. The gateman took some time to admit me through the outer curtain walls. After we were inside, he immediately shut and barred the gates again.

The city streets were eerily quiet for early evening. Finstar's hooves clattered on the cobbles and echoed back from the walls lining our route to the castle. The castle gates were shut too, but the gatekeeper recognised my voice and quickly let me through.

As I dismounted in the courtyard, Goswin ran out of the kitchen to meet me and take Finstar. Lord Heinrich received me on the steps to the Great Hall as he had done the day I had first arrived there. This time, his manner was far more cordial.

'It is good to see your safe return, Knight Gendal. Shall I fetch the Princes from their evening meal to meet you in the Lesser Hall?'

I shook my head with a smile. 'Thank you, but no, Lord Heinrich. I haven't eaten since breakfast here this morning. I'd like to see if there's any food left first.'

The Great Hall was warm and noisy with people who had eaten and drunk their fill. There was still plenty of venison, beans, root vegetables and bread left to satisfy my hunger. Heinrich gave me his own place between Oscar and Herlinde on the dais, and sat on his sister's other side.

'How have you fared, Knight Gendal?' Oscar asked.

'The traitors have wrought havoc among all the farmsteads between here and Rehschloss, your Highness,' I replied. 'Their wanton destruction is appalling: houses, barns, the harvest stores that should have kept your people fed until next summer. We need to stop them as soon as we can, before they start wrecking your vines.'

His face fell and his chin dropped onto his chest in his dismay.

A server handed me a pewter dish with a helping of venison and vegetables. Herlinde passed me some bread and offered some wine, which I refused with a shake of the head. Another server brought a goblet of water instead.

'I have also set the trap you baited, your Highness,' I said, and put a piece of venison in my mouth.

Oscar looked at me in alarm. 'I did not ask you to set a trap!'

Sinter smiled, a smug, knowing grin.

'Your brother Sigmund asked Gendal to do what should be done. You have done well, Gendal, to carry out my unspoken plan.'

'What are you going on about?' Oscar demanded, glaring at Sinter before staring at me.

'I sent a message to Opecz and Arnulf,' I said. 'The message told them where to find Brother Matthias. It was delivered by some of Silvio's band who have a grievance against Arnulf and may well turn up to watch the fray.'

'But that's appalling! You'll bring those renegades down on that innocent house of God like the wrath of Satan!'

'Don't be so pigeon-livered, Oscar!' Sinter said. 'The monastery has stout walls and ten of your household cavalry inside to defend it, as well as all the monks. You still have thirty other household cavalry here, as well as my father's escort of fifty horsemen. At most, they only have the thirty traitors who left with them.'

I shook my head and warned, 'I've heard on unreliable authority, they've gained at least twenty stateless soldiers looking for a fight, and any outlaws they have been able to persuade to support their cause.'

'Their soldiers will not be the only professionals on the field,' said Sinter.

'When do you think we should ready ourselves for their attack?' asked Oscar.

'Tomorrow by dawn,' I said.

Sinter agreed.

Chapter 28
Skirmish at the Monastery

The monastery bell tolled without a break about two hours after dawn next day. It was the signal we had expected yet feared, telling everyone in Harzberg the monastery was under attack. The speeches were now over and the time for action had come.

'They didn't start out as early as you thought, Gendal,' Sigmund said with a wry smile.

'Perhaps not, but at least we are ready,' I replied.

We were exercising on horseback at the time, out with the household cavalry in the training field. All our men at arms were in armour: mail and helmets, gauntlets and leg protectors. I was wearing my black brigandine over my mail, an extended leather helmet, and strengthened riding boots. Sigmund had also issued me with a mace and buckler, concerned that my favourite weapons of sword and dagger would not be enough. The cavalrymen also carried bucklers and maces, but their first choice of weapon for the fray would be their lances.

The cavalry rode into the courtyard and lined up in close formation, with a swift precision born of their training. Oscar's forty knights and squires assembled as a unit close to the main gates. Volkmar's fifty knights lined up behind. At the head of each cohort stood their mounted standard bearer carrying the flag of their prince: the Hart of Harzland in red on white, and the Sun of Schwarzenberg in gold on white.

The gates opened, and thirty of Oscar's cavalry rode out into the city, leaving ten of the best young knights to stay and guard their prince and his guests. Eight of the thirty peeled off in four pairs with Lord Heinrich at their head. They took the long way round to the monastery by the river road to engage the traitors from an unexpected quarter. The other twenty-two rode out of the city with Sigmund at their head to take the most direct route, intending to plough through the enemy forces at the monastery gates and trample them into the ground.

Shortly after Oscar's cavalry had left, Sinter led forty of

Volkmar's cavalrymen out of the city behind Sigmund's forces, intending to catch the enemy forces in a pincer move. Ten of these men were ready to divert as a second phalanx to the far side of the monastery walls if the situation required. The remaining ten cavalrymen stayed behind in the castle to guard their liege lord Prince Volkmar and assist Oscar's knights.

Besides the twenty knights left behind in the castle, and the eight divided between the four city gates, the defence of Harzberg also relied on the stoutness of its ashlar walls, and on the Castellan's trained militia of serfs, villeins and fief tenants. These had been called up to give military service duty as Oscar's men at arms.

I rode out beside Sigmund, on his left as we headed for the monastery. He was in good spirits and showed none of the pessimism he had voiced before Dernfels, the last battle we had ridden to together.

'If we come through this, Sigmund,' I began.

'Of course we will come through this!' he scoffed. 'We have right on our side, and all the monks' prayers for our success.'

'If we come through this, Sigmund, what do you plan to do after?'

'I haven't thought. Overwinter at Rehschloss, perhaps; hunt with Sinter; help Oscar repair all the damage these scoundrels have caused.'

'That sounds good. I am so glad you are back in the family fold.'

'You have been a good friend to me, Gendal, and I have not always treated you well. Pray, forgive me my past misdeeds. And thank you for all you have done for me: the many times you rescued me from myself, and for bringing me home.'

'The past is forgiven and forgotten, Sigmund, but I shall still treasure your thanks. Hark! I hear the war dogs baying! It's time to act like heroes for whatever we have left of this day.'

Ahead, we could hear the clamour of the marauders attacking the monastery. Our horses lumbered into a canter and then a gallop, charging into the fray with lances deployed.

The renegades were hammering the monastery's main gates with a battering ram. The ram had been made from a heavy tree trunk which took eight men to lift. Each time it was thrown, a loud cheer of encouragement went up from those waiting their turn to raise the ram. The doors shuddered with each hit, but had so far withstood their attack.

Scorch marks on the wooden doors showed the attackers had first tried to burn them down. Large puddles on the ground revealed the monks had foiled them by pouring water onto the flames from above.

Sigmund, his standard bearer and I moved aside as we approached to let the lancers through for our first counter-attack. Alone to the left of the lancers, I watched them on my right side to keep in line with them and noticed the horse of the leading lancer stumble. I looked down to see what had lamed the horse. Half hidden in the winter turf, lay some vicious metal spikes.

'Caltrops!' I shouted.

I forced Finstar hard to the left to avoid a caltrop in front of us. The turn saved his hooves but lost me my seat as he lurched round out of danger. I slid from my saddle to the ground, landing beside one of the vicious weapons. With the impetus from my momentum, I rolled away to dodge the spike and regain my feet. Then I picked up the caltrop and ran towards the lancers, waving it in warning.

The rebels saw my fall and ran from the gate to attack me. I had only the buckler on my left arm for defence and the mace in my belt to fight them off. I swung the buckler to repel their blows and wielded the mace to strike at their heads, but struggled to dodge their axe blows, which rained down on my brigandine and pummelled my mail. Their sheer force soon brought me to my knees. I fell to the ground, certain I was about to breathe my last.

Three lancers came to my rescue. They circled round the rebels, striking their heads with their maces. The rebels had to turn to fight them back or be floored themselves. The distraction gave me the chance to crawl away from the melee.

I dragged my battered body over to the edge of the trees and called to Finstar, who had gone to shelter in the underbrush. He came out whinnying in response and stood quietly as I dragged myself back into his saddle. I swapped the mace for my sword and returned to the fray. Despite my cuts and bruises and my damaged armour, I was determined to do all I could to stop the rebels.

The main fight had moved away from the monastery gates: Sigmund's forces had pushed the rebels further along the wall to avoid the caltrops littering the ground. In the shadow of the towering abbey church, seventeen of Sigmund's lancers battled with fifteen of Opecz's cavalry, warriors with red hart's heads on white surcoats fighting rebels with blue wavy lines on white surcoats. Despite their near even numbers, the insurgents were getting the upper hand, being more seasoned fighters than Oscar's men. Jousts and boar hunts could never completely prepare young knights for the vicious realities of all out battle.

As the insurgents pushed our horsemen back towards the monastery gates and the fiendish caltrops, fresh cries sounded from the road to the right. Sinter's thirty seasoned knights cantered into the fray. They fell upon the insurgents from the rear, attacking them with axes, maces and spears. The rebels bunched together for protection but had little strength left to defend themselves against the unexpected onslaught. The fresh warriors easily surrounded them and slaughtered them without mercy.

The fight was almost over when Lord Heinrich and his eight horsemen rounded the monastery walls from one direction and the ten relief cavalrymen under Sinter's command rounded the walls from the other. They picked off the handful of rebels fleeing the scene at the end of the battle. Then they gathered together near the gates to assess the scene. I dismounted close by them to pick up the scattered caltrops and make the road safe again.

By the door to the abbey church, Sinter and Sigmund congratulated Heinrich and each other, still seated on their horses. Sinter's men walked among the bodies of the fallen to make sure all the insurgents were dead. Heinrich's men carried the wounded fighters from Oscar's cavalry to the monastery for Brother Matthias to treat. Inside the monastery walls, monks showed them where to go and helped them with their burdens.

Sinter and Sigmund rode round the grisly pile of corpses lying on the road. They were counting bodies.

'There should be more than this,' Sinter said. 'How many got away?'

'None, your Highnesses,' Heinrich said; 'We watched out for them on our way here and killed everyone we came across. It can't have been more than four.'

'Then we are a good few short,' said Sigmund.

Sinter scowled. 'At least another thirty.'

I looked up from collecting caltrops to call out to them, 'And their leaders, Opecz and Arnulf'

'They've done a double bluff!' Sinter roared. 'Quick! Men of Schwarzenberg: back to Harzberg!'

'Heinrich, stay here to protect the monastery,' Sigmund ordered;

'Take charge of the men who engaged the rebels first. I will take your team of eight back to Harzberg with me.

Sinter and Sigmund left with their troops, cantering down the road to the city. Behind them, the monks came out of their monastery to welcome Heinrich and the now battle-blooded young knights.

Chapter 29
The Battle for Harzberg

The monks soon sent me back out to return to Harzberg. Thanks to the lancers who had saved me, the worst I had sustained in the skirmish was heavy bruising. I heaved my stiff body up onto Finstar and rode out through the monastery gates.

Knight Klaus followed me out on horseback and fell in beside me on my left.

'I'll race you to Harzberg!' he challenged, in good spirits now that he was free to join the fray.

'Not today, Klaus; it's my turn to slow us down. Finstar has already seen some action. I must save him for the battle ahead.'

I set the pace at a canter gentle enough for us to talk as we rode.

'That was quite a scrap!' Klaus said; 'And there we were, stuck behind the monastery walls, unable to join in.'

'Your chance will come soon enough,' I replied. 'And you did take part: you poured water on the fires they lit when they tried to burn down the doors.'

'That was the Abbot's idea. The monks formed a human chain from the well to the ramparts. The abbot got us knights to empty the buckets and jugs, as we were all wearing armour. We took it in turns to put our heads above the walls and pour.'

'Prince Sinter thinks there's been a double cross: the rebels used our ploy with Brother Matthias to lure our forces to the monastery. That's left the city with few defenders to stop them if they attack in force.'

'That wouldn't surprise me, after everything else that has happened. You certainly got a hard pounding. Why did you not just sit out the rest of the day with the monks?'

'Because it is not finished yet. There will be time enough to rest tomorrow.'

'Perhaps all too much time. It was hard just now, seeing the faces of people I had trained with, lying dead on the ground.'

'One gets used to seeing it. Pray you never get inured to it.'

'I was more surprised than inured. Do you remember I told you about that squire? The one who came with me when I brought Prince Oscar's invitation to you at Rehschloss?'

'The one who got you to steal the pots and pans to make the crash in the middle of the night?'

'Yes. I saw his face among the bodies. And he was wearing Arnulf's badge.'

'Another turncoat! How did they persuade them all to change sides?'

'Well, they didn't ask me. They probably appealed to their baser nature.'

We soon reached the walls of Harzberg and rode to the nearest city gate. I had expected to find a battle raging there and felt relieved to see an empty road outside the closed gates. I dismounted to read the scuff marks on the muddy ground. The tracks told of many horsemen entering the city, and other horsemen turning left to ride round the wall towards the East Gate.

We knocked on the studded wooden gates. The sentry peered down from a crenel in the ramparts above, half-hidden by the merlon.

'Who demands entry?' he challenged.

'Knight Gendal and Knight Klaus,' I shouted back.

He called out to the gatekeeper below to let us in. The gatekeeper quickly raised the bar and opened the left gate. After we had ridden through, he shut it again with equal speed.

Inside, the bodies of two knights lay on the cobbled square. Their torn surcoats displayed the Sun of Schwarzenberg.

'What happened here?' I asked the gatekeeper, nodding to the bodies.

'Some of Prince Oscar's men turned on us,' he said; 'They fought with Prince Sinter's men. When they killed two, the others scarpered up the hill to warn the castle. Then they tied us up and let in Lord Arnulf's men. By the time we'd freed ourselves, they'd gone up the hill too.'

'What of Prince Sinter and Prince Sigmund?'

'We let Prince Sinter in with his men not long since. They went straight up the hill to the castle as well. Prince Sigmund took his men on round outside the walls, towards the East Gate.'

I thanked the gatekeeper with a wave and cantered off up the hill after Sinter, with Klaus close behind. We arrived at the castle to find the main gates wide open.

A ferocious battle was raging in the castle ward. Mounted knights and cavalrymen were fighting each other with maces, axes and spears. On the other side of the courtyard, some thirty townsfolk fought on the steps to the Great and Lesser Halls, defending the closed doors to the royal apartments with their knife swords, cudgels and hammers.

Klaus rode into the fray at once, delighting in the chance to prove his metal at last. I decided I would be of better use going to help the occupants of the royal apartments, knowing that Oscar was not a skilled warrior and would need support to protect his vulnerable wife and guests.

I steered Finstar round the edge of the fighting, giving and parrying blows only as others brought the fight to me. When Finstar scented we were heading towards the royal stables, he needed little further encouragement from me to go straight there.

After a bit of a scrap, we managed to reach the stable doors. I rode in, ducking my head down against Finstar's neck to clear the doorway. Inside, three stableboys were trying to calm the few horses still in their care. Goswin emerged from the shadows as I dismounted. Finstar nickered in welcome. The lad ran to embrace him, tears glistening in his eyes.

'You're both safe,' he cried in joy.

'Finstar is, but he needs food and water, and treatment for his wounds. The other lads will show you what to do. I'm needed back in the fray.'

I left the stable armed with my sword and buckler, shutting the door behind me.

The battle had moved closer to the walls. I fought my way round the edge of the melee to reach the steps outside the Great Hall. The townspeople defending the steps made a space for me to join their ranks. I fought beside them for a while, pushing back those of Arnulf's men who were trying to storm the hall doors.

When Sinter's forces were gaining the upper hand at last, I turned to try the doors to the Great Hall. They did not budge.

'I need to help Prince Oscar,' I shouted to the fighting men near me.

'Try the Lesser Hall. We can't bar that door,' one called back.

A fresh wave of fighters rode into the ward from the city streets. I recognised in dismay the blue waves on the white surcoats of Opecz's men. Sigmund's cohort of Harzberg knights had chased them into the courtyard and followed them in.

The fighting redoubled. The thud and clang of weapons striking steel and wood and the shouts of men in mortal combat rose up in a deafening roar, ebbing and flowing like the sea. Such numbers of warriors were fighting in the cramped space of the courtyard, that blows against the enemy often struck both foe and ally alike.

I waited for a moment when all attention seemed to be on the fight elsewhere, and slipped away through the door into the Lesser Hall. Though the clamour continued outside, it felt a relief to be in the relative quiet of the hall. I paused to take a deep breath and weigh up my position.

As warned, I found I could not bar the hall doors shut from inside. The handles were brass knobs which would not hold a bar or chain. I looked for other ways to block the doors and tried to create an obstruction instead. The heavy table where Umbert had drunk his last proved far too awkward to push across the uneven flagstones. Instead, I dragged the two benches across the doors instead and added the carver chairs to give further weight to the obstacle.

With my back protected for the moment, I ran to check the door to the main staircase and found that locked. I pulled back the brocade curtain concealing the ladies door and found that was also locked shut. Neither budged an inch when I threw my weight against their solid timbers. I stepped back and looked up, seeking another way to access the royal apartments above. The only other opening in the walls was the musicians' gallery, but that was too high to reach without a ladder or rope. I sat down on the floor and leaned back against the wall in defeat.

'Knight Gendal, is that you?' asked a woman's deep, melodic voice from above.

I dragged myself to my feet and looked up at the musicians' gallery. There stood Herlinde, calm, composed, and dressed in her winter riding robes in case circumstances forced her to leave in haste.

'Yes, Lady Herlinde. I came to warn you that the royal apartments may soon be in danger. But I see you already know.'

'We have been watching from the solarium. Oscar has put on his sword and axe, ready to defend us.'

As she spoke, we heard the blows of men trying to break down the main doors. The makeshift barrier shifted a few inches across the floor with each push.

'I'll come down and unlock the door for you,' Herlinde offered.

'Don't! They will push it open before you can lock it again,' I shouted back; 'Hide yourself before they force their way in.'

She left the gallery and closed the door in the wooden panels. The doorway became invisible from the hall floor.

The main doors burst open, pushing the chairs and benches aside. I turned at bay, ready with my sword and buckler to face whatever came at me.

Three of Opecz's men leapt in, bounding over the obstructing furniture, They pushed it back from the door to let in others, mainly ruffians Opecz had recruited from the woods. I raised my sword to face them, certain that death would soon take me. Such lack of hope gave me a fatalism which overcame my fear and freed me to fight with an almost supernatural ability.

The rebels surrounded me with swords raised. As I parried the first strikes with my buckler, more fighters streamed into the hall, wearing the surcoats of Sinter's and Oscar's men. They set to with a great shout, coming at the rebels from the rear. My attackers were forced to turn and face them. Just one kept his back to them and swung again at me.

He was a mountain of a man, dressed in leather armour, with unkempt hair and a fixed look as he swung his battle hammer at my head. I used the advantage of my relative agility to sidestep and dodge his blows. Then I feinted and thrust my sword into the back of his thigh. He turned in rage and aimed blow after blow at me with a power that would have felled a tree. His anger forced him into more errors. As one blow passed to the left of my buckler without making contact, I came at him from the side and rammed my sword up the gap between his jerkin and breeches, cutting through his intestines as I aimed for his heart. He dropped in agony, a look of astonished surprise on his face.

To my right, Klaus was battling a knight in full chain mail with the crossed falchions of Arnulf's men on his surcoat. They were fighting with axes and daggers, and seemed evenly matched until I weighed in. I caught the man under the armpit with my sword. While the blade did not break his mail, the surprise blow distracted him, giving Klaus the chance he needed. He swung his axe across the knight's neck in a blow which broke the rings of his mail and sent him crashing to the floor. Before the knight could recover, Klaus stabbed his dagger through the gaping mail into his windpipe. The man fell back, arterial blood spurting from his neck.

'That's another turncoat done for!' Klaus cried, exulting.

We pressed on with the fight, matching blow for blow and feint with attack. Gradually, the chaos diminished around us. I looked across the hall and saw far fewer warriors still standing among the littered bodies.

Arnulf was one of those still standing, his back to the window wall. He looked tall and arrogant, with a dented helmet and a blood-spattered surcoat. Keen to honour my pledge to Silvio's people, I strode across the hall to face the traitor. Arnulf raised his sword and shield with a look of withering contempt.

'You dare to challenge me, you commoner! Don't think you'll get away a second time.'

I raised my sword in response and covered my right hand with my buckler. We circled, looking for a weakness in each other's guard. He made a slight feint backwards to tempt me to attack. I ignored his ploy and continued to circle, watching him like a hawk.

His eyes betrayed his next move before he made his first attack, a sword strike intended to disarm me. I sidestepped to take the blow on my buckler and rammed my sword between his shield and body, hoping to weaken the leather straps that held his shield. He spun round and sliced at my neck as I stepped back. Our sword blades clanged against each other. We backed off and circled again.

Arnulf was too hot-headed to wait as long as I could. He sprang in a second time, his eyes again betraying his intent before he moved. I blocked his blow with my buckler and hacked at his sword hand. Though his mail and gauntlet held, the blow would have bruised his fingers against the metal haft, and possibly broken some of them.

His next sword thrust was weaker, aimed at the side of my face where my mail ended. I parried it easily with the buckler, and circled with him again.

He lunged to my left and ran his sword between my buckler and my chest while tripping me up. I tumbled to the floor, spreadeagle with chest uppermost as I threw myself away from his blade. He raised his arms to stab my ribs with the point of his sword. I rolled out of his way and back onto my feet behind him, using my momentum to add extra power as I rammed my sword up between his legs. When I drew the blade back out, he fell to his knees in pain and disbelief.

'Your reign of terror is over, Arnulf!' I cried. 'My pledge is paid, to the people you destroyed.'

He dropped to the ground, mortally wounded, his sword falling from his hand. I kicked the blade away and placed the point of my blade against his throat to keep him down, letting him die from his wounds in agony to punish him for all the pain he had caused his many victims.

Only two warriors were still fighting when I turned back to the fray. Sinter and Opecz faced each other near the empty fireplace, the only floor space still clear. Just nine of Oscar's men and allies were watching them. They included Klaus and Sigmund.

Sinter glared at Opecz and beckoned to him.

'Come on! Try it, craven cur! Come and fight a real man,' he goaded to challenge him into opening the attack.

Opecz lunged forward with a sideswiping blade. Sinter countered with a down-strike parry as he stepped left, and struck Opecz's right wrist with the edge of his shield. Opecz swung his body round with his blade at hip height, expecting to strike Sinter's waist, but the prince stepped back again and the blade failed to make contact. Sinter struck Opecz's back where his kidneys lay beneath the bloody surcoat and mail, in a blow with the point which hurt so much Opecz spun back round to retaliate. Sinter knocked his sword out of his loose grip and kicked it away. Opecz drew his dagger, still determined to fight back; his eyes at last wide with fear.

No longer were the two fighters evenly matched. Sinter toyed with Opecz. He cut and prodded his desperate opponent with his sword and struck with his shield, in a cruel and prolonged assault which Opecz was less and less able to repel. When the prince had finally brought the traitor to his knees, he spoke.

'No-one threatens my father!'

He kicked his helpless victim to the ground, shed his sword and shield, and picked up a battle axe lying among the bodies nearby. The vicious blade swung across the air and struck through Opecz's neck to the flagstone beneath, killing him.

Sinter watched the body, the bloody axe still in his hands. When he was sure Opecz was dead, he dropped the axe and wearily strode away. Sigmund embraced him in the doorway. They walked off together out into the courtyard beyond.

Chapter 30
After the Victory

As soon as the last rebel had fallen, Oscar's servants came in to clear up after the bloodbath in the Lesser Hall. Porters took the wounded to the Great Hall for treatment. Labourers laid out the bodies of the dead in neat rows, with Arnulf's and Opecz's men below the minstrels' gallery, and Oscar's and Sinter's men by the ladies' door at the far end. I counted thirty-five bodies below the gallery. These included the two traitorous lords and also the two outlaws who had tricked me in the woods about the assault on the monastery. Fifteen lay dead on our side, most of them the men at arms who had borne the brunt of the assault for Harzberg. Their numbers were to increase as more bodies were brought in from skirmishes at the city gates and beyond.

I stood with my back to the outer wall, dazed in the aftermath: unable to move from the scene of horror that had filled my eyes. My nostrils were tainted with the metallic smell of blood. My ears were still ringing with echoes from the battle, magnified by the stone walls: the shouts and screams, the whimpers of mortal agony, the cries for mother, against the clash of metal upon metal, wood and stone. Exhaustion and shock had left me paralysed. For a while, time became meaningless. Only the carnage seemed real.

Someone spoke to me, but I could not hear them. Later, Goswin came up and took my gloved hand.

'Sir, please come with me. Finstar needs you,' he coaxed.

The thought of my beautiful horse being in need broke the spell of my morbid fixation on the carnage. I let Goswin lead me out to the stables. There with the horses, my sense of living in the present slowly returned. I gave Goswin my sword and buckler to clean, and hugged Finstar, who nuzzled me in return. His injuries were mainly superficial, and the stable lads had treated them well.

Klaus found me there later, still hugging Finstar's neck. He persuaded me to go with him to get my own wounds bandaged. Though I had come off better than many, I would still suffer the after-effects for some weeks.

At length, all the casualties had been treated, and the seriously injured transported up the road to the monks' infirmary in the monastery. Servants put the Great Hall back in order for the communal evening meal. I little felt like attending, but Klaus persuaded me to go.

That evening, later than usual, Prince Oscar's family, guests and entourage gathered for what should have been a subdued meal after the loss of so many lives and all the damage to property. It rapidly turned into a triumphal celebration of our victory. A lot of wine and beer had been drunk before the speeches were made and the meal served. When the Chamberlain called for quiet so that Oscar could address the crowd, a loud cheer went up. Oscar waited for the cheer to die down before he began his speech.

'Princes, honoured guests, lords and ladies, and all gathered here tonight, raise your cups to salute our heroes of the day,' he began.

The crowd cheered again. When they stopped to drink, he continued.

'Our gallant Prince Sinter, my dear brother Prince Sigmund for his valour at the East Gate, Lord Heinrich, Knight Gendal, and Knight Klaus! And all our brave knights and cavalry and men-at-arms, not forgetting our brave allies, the knights of Schwarzenberg!'

More cheers erupted, more toasts were drunk.

I looked along the people seated at the top table, frowning at such triumphalism. Our places had changed again to reflect our improved status as heroes of the day. Prince Oscar sat a little off centre with his wife Eleanore beside him to his left and his brother Sigmund to his right. I sat between Sigmund and Herlinde, with Heinrich and Klaus beyond her. Prince Sinter sat on the other side of Eleanore, with his mother Ilse and Prince Volkmar separating him from the Moltkés and their daughters Marlena and Aglé. The Moltkés' presence surprised me, for they had not previously graced the top table during their stay. I wondered what heroism they had performed while we were risking our lives.

Oscar saw my frown and followed my gaze as it moved over the tables below us. Many familiar faces were missing: not just those of the turncoats, but the dead and injured members of the household cavalry, men I had trained with and sparred against. Even though their spaces had been filled by Volkmar's household cavalry and the Harzland men-at-arms in recognition of their contribution to our victory, I was still all too aware of those not present. The implication was not lost on Oscar.

'Of course, we must not forget those who have made the greatest sacrifices in the defence of Harzland and our family, against the treachery of the evil Lords Arnulf and Opecz,' he said, his head dropping. 'We pray for the souls of those who died to save us, and for healing for the injured.'

Heads went down briefly.

Oscar continued, 'Much damage has been done to our lovely land by the evil perpetrators of this new year uprising: homes torched, crops and barns destroyed, people maimed and women made widows. We pledge to work with you all in the months and years ahead, to help you rebuild all we have lost. Together, we will make our beloved Harzland truly great once more!'

Cheers erupted and continued for some time, bringing Oscar's speech to an end. He ordered the food to be brought in, and the feasting began. A servant placed a trencher of the venison Harzland was so famous for, in front of Sigmund and me. We heaped slices of meat onto our plates and started eating.

'What happened at the East Gate, Sigmund?' I asked between mouthfuls.

He swallowed before he replied, 'When we arrived, the traitors were pouring through the open gates. Two of their turncoats had attacked the sentries and were letting in the rest.'

'The rebels did the same at the North Gate, but two of Sinter's men escaped them and managed to warn the castle.'

'We did our best to stop Opecz's men, and we did delay them for a time. But there were only nine of us, and my men were all unseasoned. The cavalry shook us off and swept through up to the castle. We stopped all their foot soldiers following, though. How about you? I got there just in time to see Sinter despatch Opecz, and you standing with your sword at Arnulf's neck.'

'I don't remember much, Sigmund. It is all a blur of blows and strikes. I don't know how I survived it. I do know I don't ever want to live through another battle like that again. How about you? Have your plans changed after all this?'

'Not really. I still want to overwinter at Rehschloss. I would like to do more things with Sinter – we had some great times while we were hiding at Schwarzenberg Castle. And I do want to help Oscar repair all the damage those scoundrels have done. What foul crimes they committed against us, trying to destroy this beautiful land of ours the way you say they destroyed their own. We must help all those they hurt and injured. We must bring everything back to the way it all was before.'

'Does that mean you are giving up all claim to the crown of Harzland?'

Herlinde looked across in concern. A wistful look passed briefly across Sigmund's eyes before he answered, which we both saw. He clearly realised the magnitude of the decision he was making.

'Yes, I am content to leave my brother the weight of the crown. He will abide by our father's wishes and ensure our family's succession. I was never one for politics and reading. I would rather go hunting with Sinter and adventuring with you. If Oscar should need my support, I shall, of course, always be there for him.'

Herlinde touched Sigmund's right forearm with her left hand and pressed gently to show her support for his decision. She was as aware as I was how Sigmund's magnanimity would prevent a lot more bloodshed.

Towards the end of the evening, after the servants had cleared the food from the tables, but while the wine was still going round, the Chamberlain addressed the crowd again.

'Pray be quiet for our esteemed guest, Prince Volkmar.'

Sigmund and I looked at each other in surprise as the aged prince stood up with a goblet of wine in his hand. All present followed the convention of rising with him and picking up their own drinks. Even Oscar did, out of respect for Volkmar as the most senior royal at the gathering.

'First of all,' Volkmar began, 'I wish to express my great admiration for all you brave young warriors who placed your lives in deadly peril to save our family and this beautiful country from the vile plots of evil men. A toast to all those who have survived the day.'

Drinking cups were raised and a great cheer rang out.

'And now a toast of respect for all those who fought and died this day: their names will be recorded in a Book of Remembrance, which our esteemed Dr Petrus has already started to scribe.'

Cups were raised again and cheers drowned out the second part of his second toast.

'Finally, it is my great pleasure and my wife Ilse's pleasure also, to announce the betrothal of our son Prince Sinter to Lady Marlena Moltké. We would have announced this joyful news last night, but the little matter of an uprising got in the way. Your health, Sinter and Marlena!'

Cups were raised and cheers went up yet again. This time Sigmund did not join in. Herlinde and I looked across at him. His face was ashen.

'Are you all right, Rehlein?' I asked.

'So we'll not go hunting together any more,' he said, his face vacant as if some cherished hope had died.

'Of course you will, son; just not as often,' Herlinde consoled.

'But why?' he asked.

'The events here have forced Prince Volkmar to secure his family's succession too,' she said. 'That shouldn't stop you both still being the best of friends.'

I recalled Dr Petrus saying how Sigmund's love for Sinter was like Biblical David's love for King Saul's son Jonathan, and feared a distant friendship would not be enough for him.

The company had sat down with Prince Volkmar. Sinter stayed seated to reply to his father's announcement, giving the responses appropriate to such an occasion.

'First, I must thank my parents for arranging this union for us. I must also thank Lord and Lady Moltké for the honour of pledging your precious daughter in marriage to me. We look forward to our future nuptials, on the first of May, just one year after we first met.'

The news delighted me: it meant Sinter would no longer exert his often malign influence on my friend. But Sigmund did not take it well. He grasped my hand with a force that made my bruised flesh scream in pain. I held back the cry with a deep breath.

'Cara Gendal, please don't you leave me too.'

I patted the hand that hurt me.

'I shall stay as long as you need me, Rehlein,' I pledged.

'And once we have done rebuilding, perhaps we can go questing again?'

'Perhaps. If nothing else turns up, we can ride down to Burgundy to find out whether they burnt Cara Rea as a witch.'

His hand relaxed. Herlinde discreetly slid her arm around his waist to comfort him. And I prayed that the King of Rome would not force me to break my pledge.

THE END

Thank you for buying this book. If you have enjoyed this story, please leave a review on the online book store you purchased it or on our website, www.eregendal.com using the QR code below.

We read and appreciate every one.

About the Author

Author Maggie Shaw creates her stories from her many and varied life experiences. A teenage runaway who made good before discovering her autism, Maggie writes as one who has walked the walk in recovery and spiritual development. Her degrees in science, divinity and church music, and her career as a Mental Health Dietitian, give a solid framework to the exciting adventure stories she loves to tell. The Scottish hills and Lakeland fells where her forebears farmed often feature as landscapes in her work.

Maggie is also a church musician, composer and song writer, and many of her songs are inspired by the stories she writes.

This is the ninth book Maggie has published through micropublisher Eregendal. Her music and short stories have been broadcast by Radio Carlisle, Cat Radio, and Red Shift Radio; and she has contributed articles to The St Raphael's Guild *Chrism*, The Church of England Newspaper, and *Soul and Spirit* Magazine. Online, Maggie publishes through ArtSwarm, YouTube, Sound Cloud, Facebook and the Eregendal website www.eregendal.com.

Maggie lives in Cheshire with her husband Alan and their cat Tarby.

Lightning Source UK Ltd.
Milton Keynes UK
UKHW020859271222
414464UK00014B/893